MENDING MAYHEM

FIRE WITCHES OF SALEM
BOOK FIVE

CARRIE PULKINEN

Mending Mayhem

ISBN: 978-1-957253-23-7

CHAPTER 1

EMBER

What had I done? That was a loaded question. Physically, I had vanquished a demon prince to a dark prison, saved my sister's life, and stopped the family curse from coming to fruition in my living room. Metaphysically, I'd probably caused the veil between our worlds irreparable damage and ushered in Armageddon with a slice and a jab of my sword.

Interpersonally, I'd dissolved any type of trust or bond—or whatever was happening—with Mayhem and set our journey to salvation back so far, we might never recover.

But, hey, at least Ash was back to her normal self. I hoped. "Are you okay?"

She blinked twice. "I'm fine. Are you?" Her gaze drifted down to my left hand, where Chaos's eyes were also locked. No, not my hand. They were focused on the severed head spilling blood onto the hardwood.

My brain finally received the message from my fingers, recognizing the soft tuft of hair clutched in my fist. Mayhem's body had turned to smoke when I pierced his heart, the veil opening and whisking him away to the dark prison we'd freed him from only days ago.

But his head, which I'd lobbed off in one stroke, hung from my grasp, his eyes wide with shock, poisonous blood dripping onto the floor from his neck. *Well, Ember, what now?*

"If we summon him again, he's going to kill me." I lifted my sword, resting the flat side of the blade against my shoulder. "Get a bowl. If we collect his blood, maybe we can use it in a spell to harness enough of his power for Chaos and Discord to break the curse."

Neither of them moved.

"Okay, I'll get it myself." I tried to turn around and make my way to the kitchen, but my feet remained rooted to the floor.

My head spun, the gravity of our situation reaching my nervous system and making my muscles tremble. What had I done, indeed. "I bet there's something in Chrys's dark grimoire. If we just…"

Hellfire erupted in the puddle of blood, the flames licking upward, engulfing Mayhem's severed head.

The blood on the tip of my blade incinerated, and the scent of burning hair and flesh made my stomach turn. As the fire consumed him, his skin turned to ash along with the silky locks still clutched in my fist.

His skull tumbled to the floor, the jaw disconnecting from the upper part when it thudded on the hardwood.

Damn. It looked like we wouldn't be collecting demon blood after all.

"I can't believe you did that." Ash sank onto the couch, holding her head in her hands.

I gazed at the skull. The smooth bone almost glistened in the ambient light. "That was hellfire, not witch fire."

"Not that." She jerked her hand, gesturing at me, my sword, the skull...everything in my general direction. "*All* that."

"It wasn't unexpected." Chaos sat next to her, resting a hand on her knee. "She warned him she would do it several times."

Ash tilted her head, looking at him like he'd grown a second set of eyeballs. "She vanquished him. Again."

"He was hurting you." Chaos shrugged. "I would've done the same if Ember hadn't acted so quickly."

She rubbed her temples. "He released me the second you took off his head. You didn't have to vanquish him."

"I didn't know that." Besides, what good would a headless demon do? He'd have to carry it around tucked under his arm, which would freak people the eff out. This was Salem, not Sleepy Hollow...and he didn't have a horse.

My sword suddenly felt like it weighed a hundred pounds, so I set it on the counter, my hands trembling with nothing to hold. "I was protecting you."

"Thank you," Chaos said. "You acted when I didn't. He could have caused permanent damage to her brain."

I picked up Mayhem's skull, trying my best to ignore the magical pinpricks dancing across my skin as I balanced the top part on the jaw and set both pieces on the coffee table. I lowered into a chair, my entire body convulsing as the cushion absorbed my weight. What the *hell* had I just done?

I raked a hand through my hair. "I'm sorry. I screwed up. I..."

Ash sighed. "It's okay. Luckily, he's immortal. We'll summon him again."

I nodded, words escaping me.

"Thank you," she said after a long pause. "It was scary feeling that much rage. If Chaos hadn't held me back, I don't know what I would have done."

"It was stupid." I pressed my thumb between my eyes to counter the pressure building in my head. "I never should have let him do that to you. I wasn't thinking clearly."

"I gave him permission to do it," Ash said. "It wasn't just you."

"As did I." Chaos leaned back on the sofa. "You are the first beings who have ever counteracted our magic with your own. It's new territory for us all. No need to place blame."

"Yeah." My stomach roiled, my dinner threatening to come back for an encore appearance.

"The debt he owed you has been forfeited," Chaos said, his expression grim. "When we bring him back, he'll have to help us break the curse out of the goodness of his heart, and I'm afraid nothing more than a shred exists inside him. If any."

"That makes sense. Sort of." My knee bounced incessantly, so I laid my hand on it to stop the movement. "Of course he doesn't owe me for freeing him last time...but I'm freeing him again. He'll owe me for this time, right?"

"I'm afraid not." He ran a hand down his face. "You are the one who imprisoned him. His jailer freeing him incurs no debt...merely his wrath."

"Merely." I laughed dryly. "Well, if that's all..."

Ash furrowed her brow. "But we vanquished him before, and he still owed us a debt when we summoned him. Why then, but not now?"

He nodded, looking thoughtful. "A technicality. He

had no corporeal form the first time, and you and Miles vanquished him, not Ember."

"So if I summoned him…" Ash said.

"You were here, a part of the vanquishing, no matter how indirectly," he said.

"I didn't have a clue what was happening the first time." I drummed my fingers on my knee, my thoughts racing. "Once we got him out of Chrys, my focus went to her. That's why he owed me this time. I wasn't a part of the initial vanquishing."

We sat silently, contemplating the ramifications of what I'd done. At least, I assumed Chaos and Ash were contemplating too. They weren't making goo-goo eyes at each other for once, anyway.

I stood and paced in front of the TV. "We'll get Miles to draw the sigil this time. He's even-tempered enough to work with a demon, right? Because Shade is out of the question."

Ash shook her head. "It has to be you."

I parked my hands on my hips. "I cannot deal with soulmate talk right now, so stop."

"She's correct," Chaos said. "Whether or not you are soulmates doesn't matter. Fate brought all of us together to fix this. Bringing in an outsider could be detrimental to our cause."

"It's a family affair," Ash said.

I threw my arms into the air and dropped them at

my sides. My sister, ever the logical one, was right again. Bringing Miles any deeper into the mix would be irresponsible. This *was* a family affair, and it was up to me to protect the rest of the coven from our curse.

"He's going to kill me."

She pursed her lips, giving her head a tiny shake. "No, he's not, Em."

"You don't know that." I continued pacing.

"I do, and so do you." She rose and stretched her arms above her head. "But just to be sure, you're going to bear his mark."

"The hell I am." I whirled to face her. Was she cuckoo? "Did you forget you almost *died* when you summoned Chaos that way? That Chrys *did* die?"

"Chrys and I had no idea what we were doing, and I didn't have Chaos's skull." She padded toward the hall, pausing at the threshold. "We have Mayhem's. We'll summon him into you and then exorcize him from your body to let him reform in a containment circle."

"Ash, no..." My hands curled into fists. I couldn't do it. I wouldn't.

"He'll be incapable of causing you harm." Chaos joined Ash by the hall, taking her hand.

I crossed my arms. "Yeah, right. He's probably so pissed, he'll burn through me the second I'm possessed."

"We won't give him the chance," Chaos said. "Ash will exorcize him immediately. Then, when he reforms, you won't have to worry about him killing you because you'll be connected through his mark. He'll be vanquished again if you die."

Ash chuckled. "She isn't worried about him killing her. Are you, Em?"

I narrowed my eyes, refusing to acknowledge her ridiculous statement.

"Sleep on it." She rested a hand on her demon's chest. "We have to re-summon him tomorrow morning, and you know this is the best way to do it."

"I don't *know* anything." I shifted my weight to my right leg, jutting out my hip in protest. "If we get the amulet first, we can get it over with all at once. We don't need to summon him until we find it."

"Yes, we do." She flashed a knowing smile, though what she thought she knew was ludicrous. "I'll see you in the morning, bright and early."

"Good night, Ember." Chaos followed Ash down the hall, leaving me alone with Mayhem's skull.

I eyed the hunk of bone, debating whether or not to pulverize it and be done with the insufferable demon. If my sister's life...and the lives of every witch in the coven...weren't at stake, I wouldn't have thought twice.

Much to my chagrin, however, we needed him. Dammit.

Even more chagriny...chagrinish...*annoying*... I owed him an apology. As usual, I had acted before my brain could warn me of the consequences. Hell, sometimes I wondered if I had a brain at all.

I closed my eyes, taking two deep breaths to center myself. This whole ordeal had to be one long-ass dream, right? When I opened my eyes, there would be no skull sitting on the counter, no demon in my sister's bed. Cinder and my parents would be sleeping down the hall, and I could sit on the couch and binge the last season of *Why Women Kill* like a normal person.

"As I will it, so mote it be." I lifted one lid, then the other. Mayhem's eyeless gaze stared back at me. "Oh, for Hecate's sake."

This was my life now. Might as well get used to it. I locked the door and turned off the lights before scooping up the skull in one hand, my sword in the other, and padding to my bedroom.

"You really gave me no choice." I set Mayhem on my nightstand and hung my sword on the wall before sinking onto the mattress. "I won't say I was starting to like you, but I was tolerating you better. You were growing on me."

And my body enjoyed the way touching him made me feel, despite my protesting brain.

I reached for the skull but stopped, fisting my hand and jerking it back to my lap. "What is it about you that burrows into my psyche and makes me feel things no mortal should feel for a Prince of Hell?"

My sigh came out more like a growl as I stood and headed to the shower. When I finished and put on my PJs, I opened the door and steam wafted into my bedroom, dissipating before it reached the ceiling.

Settling into bed, I turned off my lamp and brushed my fingers over the skull. It still gave me the same not-unpleasant pin pricking sensation that spiraled up my arm and warmed my chest.

"What *is it* about you?" I shook my head, attempting to chase away the intruding thoughts taking up residence in my mind, and lay back on my pillow. "If I had a type, you would be the exact opposite."

Well, personality-wise, anyway. Looks-wise... Let's just say my body wanted him to bang me like a screen door in a hurricane. "What the hell is wrong with me?"

I rolled over and put my back to him, closing my eyes and begging Morpheus to grant me a dream-free slumber. Sadly, my prayers went unanswered.

His purple eyes glittered with mischief as he trailed strong hands down my arms, turning my skin to gooseflesh. Lacing his fingers through mine, he lifted my arms before taking the hem of my shirt and tugging it over my head.

His pupils dilated, blackness spreading outward until only a thin ring of purple remained, and he inhaled deeply, his lips curling upward in approval. His tongue slipped out to moisten them, and warm shivers ran through my body in anticipation of him moistening mine.

He glided his fingertips up my stomach, cupping my breasts and brushing his thumbs over my nipples, hardening them instantly. My breathing grew shallow, every nerve in my body firing on overdrive, making my ears ring.

He moved closer, his cheek scant centimeters from mine, and he took another deep breath. A contented growl rumbled in his chest, but I barely heard it over the incessant ringing in my ears.

The culpable sound grew louder as he turned his head toward me, his nose brushing my skin.

Louder yet, the annoying sound yanked me away from him, my lids flying open, the ceiling coming into view. My breath came out in a huff, though I wasn't sure if it was irritation or relief that the dream didn't go any further.

I swiped my hand down my face and lightly slapped my cheek to wake myself up fully. Rolling to the nightstand, I grabbed my phone and answered the call. "Hello?" My voice sounded like I'd swallowed gravel.

"There's a ghost in the library," Higgins said. "Take care of it."

"What? What time is it?" I sat up and rubbed my eyes. "A ghost?"

"It's tearing the place apart. Security footage looks like it's reading some of the books too." Rustling sounded on his end. "We've never had a problem with ghosts before. Invisible bastards."

I held in my groan. "I don't think it's a ghost."

CHAPTER 2
EMBER

The needle of Ash's tattoo gun raked across my skin, the resistance to venom sigil taking shape on my arm. I winced as the ink approached the bend in my elbow, sucking a breath through my teeth.

Ash laughed and finished the final line. "All done. You should be used to this by now."

"My nervous system is fried from yesterday. From the past few months." I set the tip of my finger ablaze and lit the thicker skin, protection, and venom resistance designs, activating the magical ink. The sigil trio glowed bright red before fading to a cool blue.

"I'd ask for speed and strength too, but I don't think I can handle any more ink."

"Offensive sigils tax my vim too much. *I* couldn't

handle doing five on each of us." She wiggled her tattoo machine at Chaos. "You're up."

"I'm not sure your sigils will protect me. I'm not of this realm." He sat at her station and laid his arm on the table.

"It's worth a shot." She changed the needle and dipped it into a fresh well of ink. "The fae venom got to you last time, so we have to try."

While she applied sigils to her demon and herself, I checked my phone. I'd messaged both Miles and Shade twice, but they hadn't responded, so I dialed Shade's number, the phone ringing five times before sending me to voicemail.

"Fae are destroying the library," I said. "Meet us there ASAP."

I hit End and tried Miles. He picked up on the third ring, his voice thick from sleep. "Hello?"

"Higgins called. There's a fae soldier in the library." I assumed it was a soldier, at least. What other beastie would be invisible to the cameras? I sure as hell didn't want to know.

"What time is it?" Sheets rustled through the phone before he sighed. "It's five in the morning."

My phone pinged, and I checked the screen. Higgins's text read, *Where the hell are you? The reference section is being shredded.*

"I don't think the fae care about the time. Neither does Higgins, so wake up Shade and meet us there."

"On it," he said through a yawn. He hung up the phone, and I hoped to Hecate he didn't go back to sleep.

"They should come here first so I can give them ink." Ash lit her finger ablaze and activated the sigils on herself and Chaos. "Defensive sigil magic doesn't tax my vim as much as healing does."

"I'll let Patrice know to be ready." I sent her a text and grabbed my sword from the table. "He's tearing apart the reference section."

"Oof. We better hurry then."

I knew that would get her in gear.

She slung her bag over her shoulder and cast a forlorn glance at the tattoo mess we were about to leave behind. "We have to save the books."

With my sword sheathed in my back scabbard and four knives strapped to my legs, I led the way out the back door. If we lived in any other town, the number of weapons I wore on the daily would set off alarms. Thankfully, Salem was a booming tourist attraction, so most people assumed I was in costume.

Not that it mattered this morning. Sea fog had rolled in overnight, desaturating the dark city and making it look almost like we were walking through one of Shade's shadows. The crisp morning air raised goosebumps on my arms, and I rubbed them to chase away the chill.

"We should have worn jackets." Ash matched my

determined strides, her teeth chattering as the library came into view.

"Nah. Things are about to heat up."

My phone pinged with a response from Patrice: *Let me know if you need me. Oh, I spoke to Chrys's mom. Someone messed with the ward on her building and broke into her and a human's apartment. Could be Boston again.*

I replied: *It was us. I'll explain next time I see you. At the library now.*

It pinged again when I shoved it into my pocket, but I ignored the message and crossed the street.

Higgins stood on the front steps, his meaty arms crossed, a toothpick hanging out of his mouth. "It's about damn time you got here. You stop for breakfast along the way?"

My eye twitched. How could a man in his position hold so much contempt for the people who saved his ass on the regular? "Maybe next time you should take care of it yourself. Or are you too scared?"

"I ain't afraid of no ghosts." He ascended the stairs and unlocked the door before curling his lip at me. "But I left my proton pack at the station."

"Scrub the footage when we're done." I unsheathed my sword and stepped through the door before I could lob off his head too.

A few lights glowed softly overhead, which was all I needed to see the mess the soldier had made of the fiction section. Paperbacks and hardcovers lay haphazardly about the floor, no doubt thrown aside when the overgrown fly-man couldn't find whatever he was looking for. Loose pages littered the tables and chairs, and claw marks marred the dark wood shelves.

Ash gasped behind me. "How dare he?"

"There's a rift." Chaos marched ahead, pointing to an area on the right where a shelving unit lay on its side, the books it once contained strewn around it. "We should seal it."

A thud and a scrape sounded from above, like furniture dragging across the floor.

Ash ground her teeth. "We have to save the books first."

"Is the reference section still on the second floor?" I headed for the staircase.

"Yes," she said, and they followed me up.

As I reached the landing, I slowed, my gaze cutting left and right, searching for the *Predator* shimmer in the air, listening for the grotesque rustle of giant insect wings. The sound of footsteps echoed from below before Shade and Miles pounded up the stairs, alerting the enemy of our arrival. I held in a groan.

"You couldn't have waited five minutes?" Shade drew two knives from his harness.

"You couldn't have gotten here any faster?" I held my sword in both hands, gathering fire in the core of my being and sending the flames up the blade to illuminate the dark hallway.

"Where's Mayhem?" Miles asked.

"I vanquished him." I crept forward, my arms tensing, ready to swing at the first snap of the beastie's pincers. "Which way, Ash?"

"Wait. Seriously?" Shade laid a hand on my shoulder.

I shrugged him off. "Which way?"

"We'll explain later," Ash said before taking a deep breath. "To the left. Dammit, he's in the Salem history room. Those volumes are priceless."

My sister marched ahead, her hands fisted at her sides, and I smiled. The only time Ash Holland ever threw caution to the wind was when books were in danger.

I extinguished my sword and walked next to her, matching her determined pace. We flanked either side of the entry, and Chaos joined her, while Miles and Shade stood on my side.

One of the double doors stood ajar, and I peeked inside. Destroyed books littered the floor, their pages ripped out and shredded into hundreds-of-years-old confetti. I was never a bookish gal, but seeing our city's history torn to shreds hurt my heart.

"Someone digitized all these books, right?" I asked.

Ash's brows slammed down. "Not yet..."

Tearing paper sounded from inside, and the thud of a tome dropping to the floor followed. My sister's eyes widened.

I turned to the guys. "We have sigil protection, so we'll go in first. You two follow."

Shade opened his mouth to argue, but Ash threw the doors open and stepped into the room. "Oh, hell no," she said.

I focused my intent on recognizing the fae shimmer and followed her in to find a giant roach-man flipping through a book of historic property deeds. Of course they'd send a scout to gather information, but... "Why doesn't he show up on cameras?"

"Must be something in his DNA." Chaos gathered hellfire in his palms.

"No fire." Ash clutched his arm. "We can't risk any more damage."

Roach-man snapped his butt-ugly head toward us and hissed.

Ash held a hand toward him. "Standing tall or on—"

The fae rushed her, knocking her to the ground and chomping on her shoulder. Her sigils fought back. His teeth barely grazed her thickened skin, and her body expelled the venom in seconds.

Chaos kicked Roachman in the head, exposing his unprotected neck, and I jabbed a dagger into the soft spot beneath his ear hole. He screeched, flapping his papery wings and jetting to the ceiling before yanking out the blade. "How did you do it?"

I made a stabbing motion with my hand. "It's not hard."

He peeled back his thin lips to expose jagged teeth. "The soldier. How did you kill her?"

I laughed dryly. "Which one?"

Ash rose to her feet, the flesh wound on her shoulder already healing. "You won't find the answer in here." She grabbed Chaos's hand and nodded at Roachman.

"You will come down and allow us to kill you." He splayed his fingers, and hellfire licked down to their tips before returning inside him.

"The hell I will." He fluttered his disgusting wings, the sound making my skin crawl. "The world will be ours."

I shook my head. "You giant buggers keep saying that, but we keep taking you out. As long as witches exist, this world will never belong to the fae."

He hurled the dagger at me, the blade barely nicking my arm before it hit the ground. Yay for protection sigils.

Roachman roared and flew at me like a witch-seeking missile, slamming into my chest before pinning me against the wall. He opened his revolting mouth, venomous saliva dripping from pointy teeth, and I pressed my lips together, rolling them inward. No way in hell was I tasting that shit again.

Miles hit him with an energy ball, but it ricocheted

off his exoskeleton and hit Shade in the stomach. His body convulsed, and he doubled over, clutching his gut. "Goddess, that hurts."

"Sorry." Miles touched his shoulder.

Roachman reared back, ready to chomp my face, but I pulled the same trick on him as I had on Mayhem. Grabbing a knife from my thigh holster, I shoved it upward, beneath one of his armored plates. Sadly, I missed his heart.

He recoiled, glaring at me like I was the vilest, most insolent creature he'd ever seen. I started to tell him the feeling was mutual, but he shoved Shade aside and darted out the door before I could open my mouth.

I gave chase, barreling down the stairs after him and setting my sword ablaze. When I reached the ground floor, I swung. Fiery enchanted silver sliced into his wing, making him howl. He flapped, bits of char raining onto the floor, but he couldn't take flight.

My team closed in behind us, the guys with their weapons drawn and Ash holding three potion bottles. Roachman screeched and chittered, speaking a language that didn't even sound like words.

Ash recited a perimeter-locating spell and blew powder into the air. It collected around a two-foot rift, revealing four sets of talons trying to rip it open wider. The claws shimmered and disappeared.

"Effing soldiers. Seal it before they get through." I

swung my sword at Roachman, but he feinted left and lashed out a clawed hand, cutting into Ash's arm and knocking the second potion bottle out of her hand.

It shattered on the floor, liquid spilling around her feet, sizzling and turning into purple smoke.

"Crappity crap! That's a nerve hex." She tensed, drawing her shoulders toward her ears, her face contorting with pain.

Chaos threw a punch, hitting Roachman in the jaw. The fae careened backward, falling on his ass before hissing and darting through the rift.

An oblong shimmer protruded from the tear, and I brought my blade down, slicing through it. The cloak disintegrated, revealing a soldier's insect-like arm, and Ash wheezed, collapsing against Chaos.

"Is this the sealing spell?" I pried the last bottle from her rigid fist, and she nodded.

I tossed the bottle to Miles and let the guys take care of the rift before turning back to my sister. "Do you have the antidote?"

She nodded, patting her bag. Her knees buckled, her legs swelling, turning purple beneath her fishnets, and Chaos lowered her to the floor. I rummaged through her bag while Chaos removed her boots and tore off her tights.

"Those protection sigils don't last long enough." There must've been thirty bottles in her satchel, some individual ingredients, some premixed spells...none of them labeled. "Which one is it?"

"Red jar," she said through clenched teeth. Sweat poured down her face, and her body seized, every muscle tensing before she passed out from the pain. Nerve hexes were the worst. I knew that from experience.

"Help her," Chaos demanded, not hiding the menace in his voice.

"I am." I twisted off the lid and smeared the semi-gelatinous liquid over her swollen legs. Sparkles gathered on her skin, the purple fading to her normal pale complexion, the swelling receding instantly.

Her eyes flew open, and she sucked in a massive breath before bolting upright. "Where'd the bastard go?"

"Through the rift. He got away." I found a towel in her bag o' magic and wiped my hands.

"It's sealed." Miles handed me the empty bottle.

I returned it and the jar to the satchel. "Since when do you play with nerve hexes?"

"Shade's was so effective on us, I thought it might work on the fae." She put on her boots. "I didn't plan on dropping it."

"You should use capsules like the witches in New Orleans." Chaos helped her to her feet.

"As soon as I have a moment to breathe, I'll figure

out how to make them." She rotated her ankles and shook out her legs. "All better."

"Be more careful with those." I sheathed my sword and tucked my hair behind my ears. "If the smoke had spread to all of us, we'd be dead."

She laughed. "But you said being too careful would get us killed. Make up your mind."

"You know what I mean." I jerked my head toward the exit. "Let's get out of here so Higgins can concoct his story and deal with the mess."

The Chief arched a brow as we filed past him, expecting a detailed report but not using his words like a big boy. When I didn't give him what he wanted, he grabbed my arm. "Well?"

I looked at his hand before glaring into his eyes. "I suggest you let me go before I—"

"Ember..." Ash's voice dripped with warning, and yeah, okay... Threatening to decapitate a police officer wasn't in my best interest, but I was so goddess-damned tired of his disrespect.

"Will you please let me go?" I forced a smile, trying my best not to sneer.

He dropped my arm, and I stepped back out of his reach. "Did you kill the ghost?"

Hecate, please give me the strength to answer him without sounding like a snarky bitch. "Even if it were a ghost in the library, you can't kill something that's already dead." I crossed my arms. "The creature inside was a fae scout looking for information, and no, we did not kill him. He went back to his own realm, and we sealed the rift. Call it whatever floats your boat. The library is empty now."

That sounded okay, right?

He narrowed his eyes. "What kind of information?"

"He wanted to know how we killed his friends. Of course he didn't find what he was looking for. We keep the books about real witchcraft in our coven library."

"You'll have to show me that library."

"Not a chance." I turned on my heel and descended the steps.

The sun peeked over the horizon as we made our way back home, but it wasn't yet high enough to warm the bitter wind. My hair whipped into my face as we entered the alley behind our building, and I brushed it out of my eyes, stopping short on the back porch.

"Something feels off." I closed my eyes, opening my senses to the magic surrounding the building. Only remnants remained. "Someone broke our ward."

"Hold on." Ash cast her magic-revealing spell, and sure enough, only a few sparkles clung to the door frame. Someone had dissolved the magic meant to keep out those with ill intent.

CHAPTER 3
EMBER

My pulse thrumming, I slowly turned the doorknob. Someone had picked the lock. I held up my hand, telling my team to hold their positions, and stepped to the side as I inched the door open, ready for whatever awaited us inside to attack.

Eerie silence greeted me instead.

Ash cast her spell on the entry hall, but the only magic clinging to the walls was the residue of decades of our own work. I drew my sword, holding it down at my side as I crept inside. The library stood in its normal state of disarray, but Ash's desk, always neat and organized, held a messy stack of books and one half-open drawer. She would never leave it in that state.

"Did one of you use the desk?" I asked.

The guys shook their heads, and Ash frowned, pacing toward it and restacking the books.

"I was the last one to use it." She opened the drawer fully and rummaged through it. "Nothing is missing." She closed it and shrugged. "But I left my studio a mess this morning, so it's possible I did this. I haven't had time to keep things organized lately."

"Or someone was looking for something." I stepped into the studio. Everything seemed as we left it, but the storage cabinet had one door ajar. "Ash? Is anything missing from here?"

She joined me, opening the doors and examining the shelves. "It looks like everything is here." She moved a few items, tidying up the space.

I peeked into the darkened storefront. The layer of dust on the counter said no one had been inside for weeks, yet a sinking sensation formed in my gut. Nothing was missing so far, but something felt wrong. *Very* wrong. "Shade, Miles, check the basement storage and meet us upstairs."

"On it," Miles said.

"Do you sense any beasties in our midst?" I headed for the stairs, pausing on the first step.

Chaos inhaled, stilling as he sent out his demonic feelers. "Nothing of my kind. I don't sense anything from across the veil."

My heart joined my sinking stomach, roiling into a

tangled mess of dread. "Boston. Mayhem. They tried to find his skull before." I darted up the stairs.

I'd left the skull on my nightstand for anyone brave enough to break in to steal. With Higgins on my back to hurry up and bust his "ghost," I hadn't bothered with a ward or even a hiding place.

If someone had stolen my demon, we'd be screwed.

I ignored the partially open drawers in the kitchen and barreled through the living room. Stopping in my doorway, I gasped at the sight, my roiling innards twisting and tumbling, taking the blood from my head with them as they threatened to splatter on the floor.

"Mayhem." My voice barely registered in my ears as I dropped to my knees. "I'm so sorry."

His skull lay in pieces on the hardwood. Someone had smashed him to bits and left the fragments for me to find as a big ol' *eff you*.

Pressure built in the back of my eyes, my throat thickening as I cradled the biggest piece in my hands, hoping for the not-unpleasant pinprick sensation to dance across my skin. I felt nothing but cool bone.

"Oh my goddess." Ash grabbed an empty shoe box from my closet and helped me gather the pieces. "What happened?"

"I don't know." I counted twenty-three fragments as we added them to the box.

"Someone does not want my brother to reform." Chaos went to my dresser and rummaged through the open drawers, pushing my clothes aside. "The amulet isn't here. Did you move it?"

I opened the nightstand drawer and held up the container. "It's here."

Chaos pursed his lips, narrowing his eyes in confusion. "Did the fae hit you in the head?"

Ash's expression matched his. "That's your vibrator, Em."

"No, this is my vibrator." I held up the device in question. "*This* is an amulet with a cloaking spell." I returned them both to the drawer and closed it.

My sister nodded her approval. "Smart. Nobody would mess with that."

Chaos raised his brow. "I suppose not."

I picked up the box o' bones and sat on my bed, holding it in my lap. My lower lip started to tremble for some goddess-knew-why reason, so I bit it. My mind reeled. Who could have known the skull was here? The only people I'd told were the ones who'd been with me all morning.

I took a piece of skull from the box, running my finger over the jagged edge. "Can he still reform? We have to bring him back. We can't do this without him."

And I suddenly missed the big beast. Sure, he drove me batty and needled me every chance he got, but I wouldn't wish an eternity in the dark prison on anyone.

If I were honest, I'd admit I kinda liked our banter.

"If all the pieces are there, he can reform." Chaos eyed the floor where his brother had lain. "You'll need the debris as well." He pointed at a few pea-sized shards lying on the wood in a pile of bone granules.

"I'll get the dustpan." Ash turned on her heel and stepped through the door.

"Who would do this? Nobody knew he was here." I kneeled on the floor and picked up the tiny bits, adding them to the box. "And how will we know if all the pieces are here? I won't chance possessing myself if we can't exorcize him."

"Exorcizing him won't be a problem." Ash swept the granules into the dustpan and emptied them into the box. "But if his skull isn't complete, he'll look for another host. He tried to possess you when we exorcized him from Chrys."

"I thought he was in a containment circle." I stood and carried the box to the living room.

"It cracked." Ash followed. "His smoke poured through and circled above you before we vanquished him."

"Why am I just now hearing about this?" I set what was left of Mayhem on the coffee table and plopped into my favorite chair. Normally, news like that would have me reeling. Now...it seemed like par for the course.

Chaos shrugged. "It's not important. Do you have all the pieces?"

Not important that a demon prince tried to possess me, and it never crossed their minds to tell me. In the grand scheme of things, I supposed it wasn't. Not anymore.

The door swung open, and Shade stepped through. "The basement seems fine."

Miles followed. "It's hard to say if anything is missing, but nothing appears out of place. Whoa. Is that...?"

"It's Mayhem. Can you get the superglue?" I sat cross-legged on the floor and grabbed the two biggest pieces, turning them until they fit together. "It's arts and crafts time."

"Here." Miles set the glue on the table and joined me on the floor. "What happened?"

"That's the million-dollar question." I applied a thin strip of adhesive to one of the pieces and pressed them together, counting to fifteen for it to set before picking up another piece.

"Someone was obviously looking for something." Ash sat across from me and helped rebuild the skull.

"Yeah, but what?" I found another piece that fit. "If they were here to destroy the skull, it was in plain view in my room. They wouldn't have gone through my dresser."

"It has to be the amulet." Ash handed me a triangular piece to add to the cranium. "Maybe one of Chrys's followers knew about it."

"How would they know it was here?" Shade grabbed a protein bar from the pantry and shoved the whole thing into his mouth. "They'd look for it at Chrys's," he mumbled around the food.

"They could have scried for it." Miles tried a tiny shard in the hole on top of the cranium, but it didn't fit. "Maybe they went to her place first. Who knows?"

"Wait." I handed the partially assembled skull to Miles and grabbed my phone. "Patrice said Chrys's mom knew about our break-in. Maybe she…" I swiped open the screen and read the message I'd ignored. *Oof.*

"Someone went in after us." I swallowed the bile from the back of my mouth. "A human was murdered…gutted. A cat too."

"Oh crap." Ash set the piece of skull she was gluing on the table. "Livers?"

"She didn't say. They turned Chrys's apartment upside-down, though." I dialed Patrice's number and put it on speaker. She answered on the fourth ring.

"What else did Ivy tell you?" I asked.

"Hold on." Rustling sounded through the phone, followed by a door clicking shut. "Just what I told you. Did one of your demons…?"

"No." I shook my head adamantly, though she couldn't see my rejection of the idea. "Mayhem broke down the wrong door, but no one was home. And we unraveled the ward, but we found what we were looking for at Chrys's without tearing the place apart."

"What were you looking for?"

"She had a piece of an amulet that gave her more power." Ash glued another shard of skull. "It's how she got so strong."

"Oh," Patrice said. "That makes sense, I guess. But you have it now?"

"It's in a safe place where no one will find it." I plucked the missing cranial fragment from the box and handed it to Miles. "We have to find the rest of it before we can summon Discord."

"And before whoever else is looking for it finds it," Chaos said. "Did she tell you anything about it?"

"She never mentioned it to me," Patrice said.

"Not even in a villainous monologue when she rooted you to the basement floor?" I held the cranium while Miles glued the rest of the orbital bone into place.

"No, sorry. But the coven has sealed three rifts today, and it's not even noon."

"Thanks, Patrice." I pinched the bridge of my nose. "It's only going to get worse from here. Stay vigilant."

"We will."

I hung up and glued a tooth into a section of jawbone. "What would the fae want with the amulet?"

"If they're even the ones looking for it." Ash handed me the rest of the mandible. "It could be Boston making it look like the fae."

"Shit. You're right." I fastened the two pieces together, completing the jaw.

"The amulet grants immeasurable power to its bearer." Chaos cracked his knuckles. "The half-blooded fae prince and the High Priest of Boston would both benefit from finding it."

"Great. So it's either Ignacus the Imbecile Insect, or it's Adrian the Asshat pretending to be the Imbecile." I arched a brow at Miles. "Can you talk to Wendy and find out which?"

He closed his eyes and let out a slow breath. "For the greater good, yes. But if I have to watch her pick her nose one more time, I might put her out of her misery myself."

"Hey now. That's not what light witches are about." I balanced the top part of the skull on the jaw.

"I'm happy to do the dark work for you," Chaos said, and Ash backhanded him on the shoulder, making him laugh. "I kid."

"Uh-huh. Something's off. It's not fitting right." The skull slipped off the jaw.

"It's missing a piece. Look." Ash turned the left side toward me, and sure enough, a half-inch chunk wasn't where it should have been. "That part probably got pulverized." She ran a finger through the granules in the box.

I held the skull in my hands, staring into the vacant eye sockets. The piece could have been smashed beyond repair, as she said, but something in the core of my being told me that wasn't it. Setting Mayhem on the table, I rested one hand on his skull and put two fingers into the pile of granules, closing my eyes and letting instinct take over.

A faint pricking sensation made my palm tingle, and I focused on what was left of the demon's essence. I pictured his face, the amusement in his eyes when he goaded me, the surprise when I one-upped him with my retort.

My stomach tightened, and the urge to return to my bedroom had me on my feet before I realized I had moved, my mind's eye showing me exactly where the missing piece lay. I strode down the hall and lowered to my knees, peering under the bed. Sure as sugar, there it was, right where I'd seen it in my mind.

Strange. I'd never been able to locate stuff like this before.

I returned to the living room and held it up triumphantly. "Maybe I have a little bit of Dad's magic too."

Ash looked at Chaos, and he nodded, opening his mouth to speak before I cut him off.

"It is not more proof of your soulmate theory, so don't even try." I ignored the looks they all exchanged and glued the final piece into place. "Now he's complete. Has Wendy replied?"

"I haven't texted her." Miles tugged his phone from his pocket and typed on the screen.

I gingerly picked up the skull and laid it in the box with the too-small-to-assemble pieces. "This is all of it. I'm positive."

The moment I let go of Mayhem, the skull trembled. The pieces vibrated against each other, shaking back and forth as if every seam were a fault line. Smoke rose from the glue, spiraling upward and dissipating in the air.

Every fragment we had carefully put together crumbled apart.

"Why is it doing that?" My pulse sprinting, I reached into the box, hoping to save the pieces, but the moment I touched bone, it turned to sand, sifting through my fingers as if it had never been a solid object. "What the hell?"

Chaos leaned forward, scrunching his brow. "It's as if the glue has broken the bonds of the skull...a chemical reaction unlike anything I've seen."

"Oh, crap." Ash grabbed the tube of superglue. "Crappity crap. It's the magic."

"What magic? It's just glue." I took it from her and examined the label. It looked and felt completely mundane, but knowing my sister… "Ash, what did you do?"

She held up her hands. "Not me. It kept getting clogged, so Cinder cast a spell on it so the glue would never dry unless we wanted it to."

"She magically changed the chemical makeup." Shade took the tube from my hand. "That's genius."

"Then why couldn't we feel the magic when we used it?" Miles took a turn holding it.

"Because she focused it only on the contents," Ash said. "She can cast spells through objects."

"And we just turned all we have of Mayhem from bone to sand." I ran my fingers through the grains, and they crumbled even more, turning to a fine powder. Cinder and I would have words if we made it through this ordeal.

"What now?" Miles asked. "We can't summon him without his skull, can we? I mean, not unless someone wants to sacrifice their life so he can burn through them."

"And that is out of the question." My heart sank. How could I have been such an idiot? I'd screwed us six ways to Sunday when, if I had stopped to check on Ash after I lobbed off Mayhem's head, I would have known I didn't have to vanquish him.

Then I didn't bother setting up a ward on the skull because I let Higgins get to me.

And now, this demon…this man…who'd shown me

a shred of humanity, of vulnerability he'd probably never shown anyone else, was rotting in a dark prison because I didn't stop to consider the consequences of my actions. To realize there might be a better way to handle the situation than through violence. My chest tightened, a fist of longing squeezing my heart because, goddess dammit, I missed Mayhem and now I might never see him again.

No. No, I couldn't think that way. I would get him back if I had to go to Hell and bargain with Lucifer myself. *Whoa. Where did that come from?* It didn't matter. We needed him, and we *would* save him.

"It's still his skull." I shot to my feet and paced in front of the television. "Even if it's turned to dust, it's all there. We can still summon him." I squared my gaze on Chaos. "Right?"

"I believe so," he said.

Nausea churned in my stomach. "You *believe* so? If we're going to do it the way you suggested, I need you to be certain."

He ran his fingers through the grains. "It's still bone. It will work."

A flash of red sparked inside the box, and a stream of black smoke rose in a spiral from the center.

"What's happening now?" I dropped to my knees and peered inside. "Holy Hecate. It's turning to ash."

"Super crap." My sister blinked at me, her eyes

widening. "Ashes can't be resurrected without a phoenix spell."

"Phoenix spell?" Chaos asked.

"It's the darkest of dark. A form of necromancy." I gripped the table so tightly, my nails made indentions in the wood. "We have to summon him before his skull completely burns away. Go get the grimoire. *Now.*"

CHAPTER 4

EMBER

"Bring the box downstairs." Ash shot to her feet. "All the supplies are in my studio."

I scooped the shoebox into my arms and carried it down, my insides tying into knots with each step I took. The bone powder glowed red as the burning spread from the center outward. By the time I reached the studio, half of it had turned to ashes.

"Here's the containment spell." Shade picked up the grimoire. "Does everyone remember it?"

"We don't have time for that." I poured a ring of salt and set the box on the floor as I kneeled to draw Mayhem's sigil. "And we don't have time to do it your way," I said to Ash.

"This is dangerous." She set candles at the five points of the pentagram and lit them with her magic.

"Do you have a better idea?" I drew his mark from

memory, the familiar pin-pricking sensation dancing up my arm as I completed the final swoop.

"It must be done," Chaos said.

I set the shoebox on top of the sigil and rose, dusting my hands against my pants before scanning the summoning spell. We joined hands around the circle in our usual positions, and the smoke thickened in the box, the bone burning until only a thin ring remained.

"Hit me with all you've got." I squeezed Chaos's hand, and he opened to me, a blast of demon magic surging through my psyche and making my head spin. I gave some of it to Shade, and we recited the incantation in unison.

Still clutching each other's hands, we stared at the box, waiting for Mayhem's purple smoke to consume the bone powder.

Nothing happened.

"Try again." Panic tinged the edges of my voice, and my stomach felt like it was crawling into my chest.

We cast the summoning again. Still, nothing happened.

"It's not working," Ash said.

"No shit." I focused on the sigil, an image of Mayhem's face forming in my mind. "One more time. Don't hold back."

Another tidal wave of magic coursed through my system, the essence of three other witches and a demon spiraling through me, mixing and melding until I thought I might burst. "Hecate, please help us."

We recited the summoning a third time, and I reached as far into the ether as my mind would allow, searching for the low vibration of my demon. I found nothing, and the black smoke in the shoebox faded as the last of the bone powder incinerated, leaving behind a single glowing ember.

Shade loosened his grip on my hand, but I held him tighter, refusing to give up. This had to work. Mayhem had to come back.

"Please," I whispered. "I need you."

The final ember dimmed, taking my hope with it.

My posture deflated, and I dropped my hands to my sides. Pressure built in the back of my eyes, but I blinked back the tears threatening to fall. I would not get emotional in front of my team. Not now. Not ever.

I strode to the table and slammed the grimoire shut. "I'm sorry, Ash. I..."

"Ember..." She grabbed my arm and spun me toward the summoning circle.

A thick stream of purple smoke poured through an invisible rift, billowing inside the ring before swirling around the box. My breath caught at the sight, and I pressed a hand to my chest. My heart sprinted beneath my fingers as I stepped toward him, a mix of relief, wariness, and elation swirling inside me.

"Mayhem?" I reached for the demon.

He recoiled, his face forming in the smoke. "You burned my skull?"

"It was an accident." I held up my hands. "We were trying to bring you back."

"Liar!" He slammed into my chest, and I careened backward, crashing into the wall. An arm formed, pressing against me with nearly enough force to crack a rib, his smoky face two inches from mine as he spoke.

"Now I cannot reform without a host," he growled.

I shook my head, wheezing as I sucked in a breath. "We'll figure something out. Give us some time."

His lip pulled into a sneer. "I cannot exist in this realm without a corporeal form. You, dear witch, just condemned one of your coven members to death."

His smoky form jerked away, billowing toward the door.

"Take me." I stepped toward him. "I'll be your host."

His menacing laugh echoed as if it had formed in the bowels of Hell and traveled across the veil the moment he opened his mouth. "I will deal with you after I reform."

He shot through the door, knocking the books off Ash's desk on his way out the back, and all I could do was watch him leave.

Silence filled the room like someone stuffed it with cotton, no one moving a muscle as what just happened sank in. My mouth hung open, so I snapped it shut and waited for my brain to process it all. The skull was gone...completely ash...before Mayhem crossed the veil.

"How...?" I turned around to find my team with the same perplexed expressions. "There was nothing left. The skull was mostly ash when we started. We shouldn't have been able to bust him out of prison without it."

"*We* didn't." Chaos leaned against the table and crossed his arms. "You did."

"No." I picked up the box of ashes and set it on the table. "We all recited the words. We shared our magic."

"If that was all it took, it would have worked the first time." Ash picked up the candles, extinguishing them one by one. "Any chance of using his skull to summon him died when the last grain went out. Hell, we probably lost our chance when it first started burn-ing. This was all you, sis."

I shook my head. It didn't make sense.

"Did you do something different the third time we tried?" Miles swept the salt ring into a dustpan.

"No." I racked my brain, trying to remember, but the adrenaline from getting slammed against the wall by a smoke demon hadn't dissipated from my system. "I don't think so."

"You connected with him through the veil," Chaos said. "I felt it happen."

"I didn't... How?"

"The same way Ash connected with me. Through your bond." He set the salt canister in the cabinet. "You are two halves of a whole."

"Then why wouldn't he possess her?" Shade asked. "Not that I wish it on her, but wouldn't he want to burn through Ember and bring the two halves together for good?"

"They're soulmates," Miles said. "Of course he wouldn't."

"Do you believe us now?" Ash carried her tattoo machine to the table and pulled up two chairs. "Only you could summon Mayhem without his skull, just like only I could summon Chaos."

Shade laughed, disbelieving. "I supposed that means Cinder..."

"And Discord, yes," Chaos said. "The six of us coming together was written in the stars long before any of you were born."

I looked at Chaos and then my sister, who raised her brows, giving me her *get over yourself and accept it* look. "You feel it," she said.

"I don't know what you're talking about." Yes, that was a lie. I did feel it, all the way down to the core of my being, swimming in my blood and penetrating my bones.

It didn't mean I had to like it.

"Come on. Sit." Ash poured magical ink into a well and sat at one of the chairs. "You need to catch your demon before he hurts someone else."

"What are you thinking?" I took the chair across from her. "I'd say speed and strength, but I don't think those would help with wrangling a giant puff of smoke."

"No." She dipped the needle into the ink. "You're going to make him possess you."

"You're the only one who can survive it," Chaos said. "He'll hold back as long as he can while you formulate another plan."

Ash swiped open her phone and pulled up Mayhem's mark. "And if we can't reform his skull, we'll exorcise him and send him to prison. We won't let him hurt you."

"I don't need convincing." Because I would not sacrifice a coven member...or anyone else...to bring him back. I laid my arm on the table. "Let's do it."

"Focus on Mayhem while I draw it. Don't think about anything else." She pressed the pulsing needle against my skin. "Picture him in your mind and feel the emotions he stirs inside you, whatever they are."

That was easy-peasy. The infuriating, sexy-as-hell demon hadn't left my thoughts since the moment he arrived. I closed my eyes, imagining the way he looked at me, feeling the adrenaline spiking in my system every time he tried to put me in my place. Even when his smoky form had pinned me against the wall, my fear had bled into...arousal?

Gross. No, that wasn't the right word. Excitement, maybe.

I was so lost in thought, I didn't feel the tattoo until Ash reached the delicate skin on the inside of my wrist. I winced at the burning, stinging sensation and opened my eyes. "Don't forget it goes left."

She chuckled. "I won't."

With the final loop complete, Ash turned off her machine and carried it to the counter. She wiped the excess ink from my skin before admiring her work. "It looks good on you."

I agreed, but I didn't dare say it aloud. "Is there anything special I have to do before I activate it?"

"I don't think so." She emptied the ink well and washed it in the small sink next to her supplies. "I had no clue I was summoning a demon when I did it."

Chaos laughed. "She wanted help organizing her library."

"Which we will do when this is all through." She wrapped her arms around his waist and nodded at the sigil on my arm. "It's time."

I took a deep breath, centering myself. "Let's light this baby up."

CHAPTER 5
MAYHEM

Betrayal didn't begin to describe what Ember had done. I growled as I flowed out of her home, reining in my smoke to blend with the air around me...the one and only benefit of this fluid form. I had only hours to find a host before the dark prison sucked me back across the veil, trapping me in nothingness for eternity.

How could that witch...my soulmate...do this to me?

In the time I'd spent alone, devoid of all my senses, with nothing but my thoughts to occupy myself, I had resolved to forgive her. Ember and her sister had a special bond. Of that I had no doubt.

I also had no doubt that my brother would have torn off my head and clawed out my heart had Ember not acted so quickly. I much preferred her blade to Chaos's talons.

Her decision to end my time on Earth had come from a place of love and devotion, and I would have expected nothing less of her. I had hoped that, perhaps one day, she would find in herself the same love and devotion for me.

Instead, she destroyed my skull and then summoned me back to torment me with her betrayal.

How could I have been so stupid?

It was Isabel all over again, yet this time, for some reason, the witch's treachery cut deeper than I ever could have imagined.

My mission now was simple: Find the strongest witch in the coven—after the three involved in Ember's villainous plot—and possess and burn through him, gaining as much power as possible. I would steal the amulet shard to increase my strength and put an end to the Holland bloodline.

Then, I would take out my brother too. Damn him for his involvement.

I poured down the main street, opening my senses and searching for the high vibration of witchcraft. I had met their healer, Patrice, but she was far too weak. I wouldn't waste my time on anyone who only possessed such passive magic.

My first choice would have been their shadow witch, had he not been involved in the destruction of my skull and the resummoning. Miles, with his under-developed energy manipulation ability, would have been my second choice, but both men needed to suffer along with the women.

Humans lurked about everywhere, peering into windows and snapping photos with their phones. Even with the threat of a serial killer in their midst, they risked their lives to post their images and measured their self-worth by how many others liked them.

Idiots.

The only reason the species had survived so long was because their damned souls provided the most potent fuel in the Underworld. Lucifer knew I'd take pleasure in eradicating them otherwise. He'd threatened to end my existence multiple times because of it.

I traveled out of the downtown area and headed toward a residential section of Salem. Surely, I would find powerful witches living amongst the mundane here. A tickle of energy pulled me to a white building with blue shutters on the windows. I stilled, absorbing the essence of the being inside, sifting it through my metaphorical fingers to gauge his power. He was nothing more than a kitchen witch.

I moved on, searching and feeling until a sharp spike of magic gripped my psyche. I fought it, certain the dark prison was already calling me home, but the power was too great, the pull too strong.

This wasn't the prison. No, the vibration was too high to have come from Hell. Before I could contemplate it more, the energy ripped me through the fabric of reality and slammed me into the mind of the one who had summoned me.

Darkness engulfed me. Then piercing white light blinded me. Raw elemental magic, stronger than any I had felt before, surged through my soul, enrapturing me. I reveled in it, rolling in the power like a hellcat in a field of catnip, feeling as though, at last, all the missing pieces of my existence had snapped into place.

My host blinked, her vision still blurred, and she clutched her head. "Whoa. My skull feels like it's going to crack open."

Her warm honey voice soothed me, tempering my rage as I opened myself to all her senses.

"Hold on. I have a spell for that," a familiar voice said. "Shade, slide that trash can over to her. She'll need it."

My host's stomach retched. She dropped to her knees, clutching the rim of the bin, and vomited. Her last meal mixed with bitter acid, burning her throat, and bringing me to my senses. Of course it would be her. No one else would be strong enough to force a demon of my level to possess them.

"Ember..."

"You don't have to shout. You're literally in my head." She accepted the napkin and water Miles offered, taking a sip and swishing before spitting into the bin and wiping her mouth.

"Here." Ash set a grimoire on the floor beside her. "Cast this one. It doesn't require a potion."

Her vision swam, tears blurring her eyes. She blinked them away, bringing the page into focus. "May the light of the goddess lift my pain. My headache will ease like a cleansing rain."

She sat back on her heels and rolled her neck as the pressure eased into a dull ache. "I seriously thought my skull was going to split."

The fury, which her essence had eased in me, returned with a vengeance at her words. *"You dare mock me with talk of your skull after you destroyed mine? I should burn through you right now and take Salem as my own."*

She rose to her feet, gulping down the rest of the water as Miles whisked the trash can out of the room. "You need to calm your hysterics, buddy. If you make my headache come back, there will be hell to pay."

"How dare you tell me to be calm? I demand you release me immediately."

She sucked in a breath through her teeth. "First of all, I'll release you when I'm damn well ready and not a moment before. And second... It doesn't feel good to have your emotions dismissed, does it?"

"The witches have a plan to help you reform

without killing a host," Chaos said. "But you must remain inside Ember until it is complete."

"Treacherous witch. You destroyed my skull."

"I told you that was an accident. Now, hush so I can think." She paced the length of the room.

"You speak with a forked tongue. It was no accident."

She sighed heavily. "Chaos, will you tell your brother we didn't do it on purpose? The vanquishing, yes. I meant to do that, but I planned to bring you right back."

"It's true." My brother looked into her eyes, squinting as if trying to see me in her irises. "We were called away to battle a fae. When we returned, your skull had been pulverized."

"And burned to ash. Only magic could have destroyed it by fire, and you are the only fire witches in Salem."

"He's saying only we could have burned it." She pressed her fingers to her temples. "We don't have time for this."

"We did burn it," Ash said, "but I promise it was an accident."

"We were trying to glue it back together," Miles said as he returned to the room. "We didn't know Cinder had enchanted the glue."

"Come on. We've got research to do." Ember strode out of the studio, stopping in the library by Ash's desk.

"What kind of enchantment?"

"It dissolved the bonds holding the bone together.

After your skull turned to powder, it started smoking. We rushed to summon you before it burned out, but we were too late."

I remained silent, contemplating her story as the others joined her in the library. A large part of me desperately wanted to believe her, but hope belonged to the inexperienced youth. History had proven, time and again, that witches could never be trusted.

"A phoenix spell." She stood facing the desk, drumming her fingers on the surface. "Do we have one?"

Ash screwed her mouth to one side and sank into the chair. "There could have been one in the dark grimoire Mom and Dad gave to the demon."

"A lot of good that does us now." Ember strode to a bookcase and ran her finger through the dust on a shelf. "What about in the ones we took from Chrys or the teens who summoned the shedim?"

"It's worth a shot. Let me grab them." Ash rose and strode to the back of the library.

"Tell me about this phoenix spell. What is your plan?"

"It's dark magic, a type of necromancy...and it's forbidden."

"We know that," Shade said.

"I'm talking to Mayhem." Ember tapped her temple. "If we can find one, we can use it to resurrect your skull and bring you back to the land of the living."

"And face the wrath of the Higher Power if they

find out." Shade picked up a book from a stack on the floor and flipped through the pages before tossing it onto a shelf. "I'm not a fan of this idea."

"You don't have to help." Ember dropped into the chair and crossed her ankles on top of the desk. "But there's no other way to do it. I refuse to sacrifice a living being."

"What is the punishment if your Higher Power catches you?"

She shrugged. "A few years in prison at best. At worst, we could be killed...or stripped of our magic and banished to Arkansas." Her body shuddered.

"You would take that risk to save another witch's life?"

"And to save yours. As long as you behave yourself, that will be the last time you go to the dark prison. You're starting to grow on me." Her breath caught as if she didn't mean to say the last words aloud. "Like a fungus, I mean."

She peered at her arm, where my mark glowed a soft red, and ran her finger over the sigil. The sensation felt like warm silk running through my psyche and caressing every inch of my nonexistent body.

"Mmm... I like that."

She jerked down her sleeve.

"I'm not sensing a phoenix spell in either of these." Ash returned with two grimoires clutched to her chest. "I'll double-check to be sure."

Ember stood, giving her sister access to the desk. "If you don't sense it, it's not there."

"I still need to look. It's a forbidden spell, so it could be cloaked." She opened one book and pushed the other toward Ember. "Check this one."

Ember flipped through the pages, running her fingers over each entry. I felt her psyche open to the energy around her before she focused it into the grimoire. Her magic called to me, my demonic form begging me to take it as my own.

But the man in me didn't simply want her power. I wanted everything. Her body, her heart, her soul. My raging fury cooled to a slow simmer, but I had to be certain of her intentions before I extinguished it completely.

"I believe I can remain inside you for two weeks without burning through your form. If you focus on finding the amulet, you can summon Discord and we can lift the curse without risking your life and your magic."

She sighed. "Not a chance, Your Royal Pissiness. I did this to you. I'm going to make it right."

Hope sprung alive inside me once more as she perused the pages, ready to risk everything to save me from the dark prison. Perhaps her words were true. Maybe my skull's destruction really was an accident.

"I don't sense any cloaking magic in this one. Trade?" She closed the book and turned it toward her sister.

"Nothing in here either but check again." Ash handed her the grimoire. "Better safe than sorry."

"What about you? Do you feel anything that could be masking or cloaking a sinister spell?" Ember turned the page.

"I'll give it a shot," Shade said.

"Mayhem?" Ember turned another page. "Do you feel anything through me?"

I focused on the coarseness of the parchment beneath her fingertips, searching for energy in the ink. *"I do not."*

She stepped away from the book, and Shade flipped through the pages. "I highly doubt we'll find one on the witchy web."

"It's worth a shot." Ash typed on the keyboard. "I'll use a double-encrypted browser to search."

Her fingers flew across the keys as she chewed her bottom lip. A few minutes later, she slumped in her seat. "Nothing. No one would advertise it if they had one."

"I'd bet my left boob someone in Boston does. We can't risk breaking into their library again, but do you think you could sense the spell if we walked the streets? Maybe we could borrow one from a dark witch."

"You're overestimating your sister's ability. Take me to their High Priest and allow me to burn through him. It will solve two of our problems."

"Zip it, dude." She tapped her temple.

Ash inhaled deeply, a look of uncertainty furrowing her brow before she wiped it away and nodded. "If there's a phoenix spell in Boston, I'll find it."

"Fabulous. Another side quest." Ember rubbed her forehead. "I hope we can at least battle a beastie along the way."

CHAPTER 6
EMBER

After a morning fae fight, a demon summoning, and then my possession, I was famished, so we stopped for burgers on our way to Boston. Miles paid the tab this time and thank the goddess for that. Hecate knew I wasn't the best at saving, and my credit card would be maxed out soon.

With all the paranormal shit going on in our lives, it was easy to forget the normal. Thank the goddess for that too, because getting caught up in my head, thinking about finding another job and paying the bills right now, was the last thing I needed to worry about.

We had much bigger insects to fry at the moment.

Shade took the wheel, with Ash riding shotgun, and I sat in the middle seat with Chaos on my right and Mayhem in my head. They didn't trust me to drive with a violent demon chattering in my psyche. Imagine that.

The deep oranges and reds of the trees preparing to shed their leaves whizzed past as Shade drove faster than necessary, but who was I to complain. If anyone had a sense of urgency on our current quest, it was me. Ash lasted as long as she did with Chaos in her head because he held back.

After everything I'd done to Mayhem, I doubted he'd show me the same courtesy.

"Park over there. It's better if I walk." Ash pointed to her right, and Shade turned, rolling to a stop at the curb.

I climbed out and opened the hatch in the floorboard before handing an extra set of knives to the guys. "Better safe than sorry." I grabbed my sword.

Miles arched a skeptical brow. "I hope you have a cloaking spell for that. I don't think you can get away with carrying a weapon in plain view in Boston."

I pursed my lips and eyed my beautiful blade. Shade could put it in a shadow, but if something happened to him, his magic would dissipate and it would be in plain view. "Do you have any cloaking spells in your bag o' tricks, Ash?"

"They're too volatile to carry premixed." She slid out of the passenger seat and closed the door.

"You'll have to sit this one out." I laid my sword in the hidey hole and latched it shut.

"You don't need it. Between your fire and your fighting skills, you are unstoppable."

I laughed. "Should I take that as an actual compliment?"

"It's the truth. Take it however you need to."

"It was a compliment." My mouth threatened me with a smile, but I fought it. Mayhem's opinion of me shouldn't have mattered. It *didn't* matter.

Ash grinned, and I rolled my eyes.

The guys put on jackets over their knife holsters, and I did the same. Ash stood on the sidewalk and closed her eyes, doing her magical thing, and I couldn't help but smile this time.

Pride swelled in my chest. My little sister had turned into the most amazing witch in a matter of weeks. At least one good thing had come out of this ridiculously terminal ordeal.

"What do you feel?" I asked.

She shuddered. "Icky, sticky dark magic."

"Obviously." I hadn't even opened my senses to it yet, but I could feel it dampening the air and clinging to my skin like a wet sock. Yuck. "What about the spell?"

She shook her head. "Let's walk."

"Boston is almost 90 square miles." Shade strode

beside me as we followed Ash and Chaos. "It'll take forever to walk it all."

"We won't have to," I said. "Ash directed you to park in this end of town for a reason."

"It's just a hunch," she said.

"We both know it's more than that." I rolled my shoulders, missing the feel of my sword on my back.

"What is this emotion you're feeling?"

"What does it feel like?" I asked.

"Nothing yet." Ash turned down a side street, and I followed.

"Sorry. I'm talking to the demon in my head."

She laughed. "Now I know how you felt."

A low growl rumbled between my ears. *"If I knew how to name it, I wouldn't have asked."*

"Physically, I mean." I tapped my temple when Shade cut his gaze to me. "Mortals are complicated creatures. Lots of emotions."

"It's pleasant. Your chest feels full. Your lips curve upward, but you're not quite smiling anymore. It seems to be directed toward your sister."

"I'm proud of her. If you'd met her before everything started, you'd see how much she's grown." The full feeling in my chest and my smile were also the result of having him back, but I didn't dare say that out loud.

Yeah, okay, fate had brought us together. I believed it now, no matter how badly I wanted to deny it. After summoning him without his skull...all by my lonesome, apparently...fate was the only explanation. It wasn't logical in the slightest, but logic was Ash's jam.

Action was mine.

Chaos stopped abruptly and grabbed Ash's hand. "I sense a rift."

"As do I."

"Mayhem does too. Where?" I reached into my jacket, wrapping my fingers around a dagger.

"To our right."

"This way." Chaos turned down the street, and we strode toward a massive red brick church with a white steeple.

A four-by-three-foot gash in...the veil?...hung to the left of the building, its edges rimmed in glowing orangish-red.

"Whoa." I stopped and rubbed my eyes, expecting it to vanish from sight, but it stayed there, suspended in midair.

A ripple darted from right to left, and a six-foot-tall beastie with goat horns and the face of a hyena barreled toward it. Four witches gave chase, one of them hurling a blue ball of energy toward the ripple. He missed—fae soldiers were fast AF—and hit the metal fence surrounding the churchyard, electrifying it. It sizzled and popped, raining sparks to the ground before going out.

Thank the goddess nothing caught fire.

"Why are they doing this in broad daylight?" I picked up my pace. "Do they not have a shadow witch?"

"Doing what?" Miles asked, matching my strides. "I don't see anything."

"You don't see the giant rift right there?" I swung my arm toward it. "And the witches trying to fight a fae soldier and a hyena man?"

"I can see through shadows," Chaos said. "She must be channeling Mayhem's power to see through them as well."

"That is precisely what is happening."

"We have to help them." I jogged toward the fray.

"How? We can't see them." Miles ran to catch up.

"I can," Shade said, matching our pace.

I cut him a sideways glance. "Since when?"

"It's an active power. I have to focus to use it, but now that I know there's a shadow here, I can see through it."

"And you never bothered to share that bit of information?" I made a mental note to take inventory of everyone's hidden talents if I ever had the time.

"I'm the only shadow witch in Salem. I never have to use it."

The battle rounded the corner, and I stopped, holding up a hand. "We'll tell them Chaos and I have that power too. They can't know about the demons."

"You need to find the phoenix spell. Let the Boston witches take care of Boston. It's not your job."

"These rifts are happening because of us. That makes it our job." I strode toward a witch who rummaged through a bag, no doubt looking for a freezing spell. "It looks like you guys could use some help."

She snapped her head up, her eyes widening before she shot another woman a chastising glare. "Gray! Our cloak."

"What? It's still in place." Gray looked me up and down. "How can you see through it?"

"It's an active power," I mimicked Shade's words. "I have to focus to use it."

Shade gave me the stink eye. "I have it too."

"As do I," Chaos said. "If you will bring the other two into your shadow, we will assist you."

The soldier rippled toward us, and I threw a fireball, slamming it into his chest. He screeched, his cloak slipping just long enough for me to see the paralyzing venom dripping from his pincers.

"Holy Hecate," Gray said. "Olga, she's a Holland."

"No shit," Olga said. "Hey, Adrian. We've got company."

The High Priest whirled toward me, his brow slamming down over his deep-set eyes. "What are you doing here? We don't need your help."

"Ah!" The fourth witch flew backward, his shoulder slamming into a wall before a massive gash formed in his neck. The hyena man lashed out a taloned hand, slicing into the invisible fae's soft spot.

Bug-man screeched again, dropping the witch and turning on the beastie.

"Are you sure?" I scrunched my nose. "It kinda looks like you do."

His chest puffed as he straightened his spine. "I'm sure."

I nodded toward his fallen witch. "Do you have an antidote for that? We do."

"I haven't found anything that works," Olga said.

"My sister can help him if you'll bring her into the shadow."

Gray rolled her fog outward, enveloping Ash and Miles. They darted toward the fallen witch and administered the antidote while the hyena man railed on the fae. Adrian shot me a steely glare before swirling his hand in the air, creating a little tornado and sending it toward the beasties. It caught the hyena and whirled him around before throwing him three yards away.

"Adrian is an imbecile. If he were wise, he would allow the alastor to kill the fae."

"Alastor?" I asked.

Olga flashed a puzzled look. "That's Adrian, our High Priest."

"An alastor is an upper-mid-level demon. They are skilled fighters and despise the fae almost as much as I do."

"The hyena man. It's an alastor demon," I said, quickly recovering from my faux pas. "You should let it kill the fae."

"How do you know what it is, *light witch*?" Adrian's words dripped with more venom than the fae's pincers. "Why don't you go plant a flower or make some tea? This is our battle. Leave the fighting to the real witches."

I narrowed my eyes. Leave the fighting to the "real" witches? Oh, no he didn't.

I gathered fire in my palms, bringing them together so the flames danced between them, growing bigger and hotter with my anger. I could show him a real witch. "How many fae have you killed, *dark witch*?"

Mayhem's growl rumbled between my ears. *"Now this is an emotion I'm familiar with. You should rip him open and burn him from the inside out."*

Mayhem's magic bled into my veins, and if I'd been anyone else, I would have done exactly that. But I was me. His soulmate. The only being in existence who countered his magic, and, much to my chagrin, the desire to roast Adrian's chestnuts on an open fire dissolved, taking my anger with it.

"As much as I hate to admit it, we're on the same side." I hurled my flames at the fae, but his exoskeleton shielded him, as usual. "And those suckers are fireproof."

"Which must mean you haven't killed any either," Adrian said. "At least I took out the demon."

"Don't let him speak to you that way. Tear off his head and piss down his throat."

"We're on the same side," I said again. "If we work together, we can share information. I'm sure you know things about the fae that we don't, and vice versa."

Mayhem growled in my head. *"It's me. My magic is seeping out of my psyche and making you docile. This isn't you, Ember."*

Holy crap. He was right. I mean, I wouldn't urinate on a foe—no matter how big his ego—but never would I ever let a man talk to me like I was a dainty, useless little girl. Flowers and tea, my ass.

Mayhem pulled back, the oddly calming energy he'd forced into me dissipating, and I gasped.

"Light witches couldn't possibly know more about this than we do," Adrian said.

Olga raised her hand. "Don't demons disappear when they die?"

"I'm no demon." Bugman charged her, and she screamed, ducking behind her High Priest. Chaos blocked the fae's path, landing a punch to the side of his face and breaking off a pincer. He squealed and hissed, stumbling back to where the alastor lay motionless after Adrian's tornado.

I highly doubted a little wind knocked a demon unconscious. Most likely, Chaos was keeping it in check, but I'd let Adrian have this one. If he knew we were in cahoots with the Princes of Hell, we'd have to fight off BSM too.

And we didn't have time for more side quests.

Seriously. No. More.

Ash joined hands with Miles and Shade and hit the fae with a killer freezing spell. Well, not *actually* killer, but the bugaboo's body seized, the blood from its mouth stopping mid-drip as it toppled to the ground.

"Whoa," Gray said. "How...?"

Adrian scoffed and crossed his arms. "It won't hold."

I could feel Mayhem's desire to rip his heart out growing in my mind, so I clenched my teeth and grabbed a dagger from my scabbard. "Let me do this," I whispered as I marched toward it. "You're killing my instinct to fight."

"Sorry." He reeled it in again, and my own anger surged through my veins.

I hurled the dagger at the frozen fae, the blade penetrating the soft spot below his ear hole.

"Gray and I will seal the rift," Olga shouted.

I whirled around, my expression livid. "Don't."

"Okay." She raised her hands, dropping a potion bottle and shattering it on the pavement.

"We don't take orders from light witches," Adrian said. "Seal it."

"That was my last spell. I'll have to mix another one." Olga dropped to her knees and rummaged through her bag.

I mouthed the words *let the alastor go* to Chaos, and he nodded, releasing his hold on the demon. The beast charged toward me.

CHAPTER 7
MAYHEM

"H is heart is lower than a human's, on the right side of his stomach."

"Roger that." Ember dropped and spun, kicking her right leg out and knocking the alastor off his feet. He hit the pavement face-first and howled, rolling to his back and clutching his bloody snout.

"Impressive move. You'll have to teach it to me when I reform."

"Gladly." She yanked the dagger from the fae's neck as the alastor rose to his feet. Poisonous blood dripped from his nostrils, and he shook his head, splattering it around him.

"Don't touch his blood."

"I didn't plan to." She marched toward the alastor,

the dagger at her side, ready to thrust it into the fiend's heart, and for a moment, I felt remorse.

The alastor would easily slip through the rift and return to the Underworld at my command, but I understood the need for anonymity. Even dark witches despised demons they couldn't control.

Ember's grip tightened, her muscles coiling for the strike, but the imbecile High Priest created another tornado and sucked the alastor away before she could thrust her blade.

"Are you effing kidding me?" Anger surged through her veins, and I reveled in it.

Any doubt that the universe created this witch for me dissolved as she tossed her dagger, handle over blade, and caught it, adjusting her grip and striding toward the High Priest.

"We can take care of the fae," Miles said.

"Don't," she nearly growled. "I'll handle it."

"Kill the High Priest. Take the Boston Society of Magic as your own."

"I don't want Boston." She slowed her pace. "I don't want to fight."

Lucifer have mercy. I'd bled into her consciousness again. I couldn't help myself. Being inside this warrior goddess while she battled her enemies created a feeling of elation I'd never experienced before. Tensing as much as a disembodied entity could, I pulled my magic back, gathering it into a ball of menace and tucking it into the recesses of my consciousness.

She gave her head a hard shake, regaining her senses and continuing her march toward the foolish High Priest. "What are you going to do? Wind him to death?"

Olga cowered on the ground with her spell kit while Gray strained, her face pinching with the exertion. "I can't hold the shadow much longer."

"I'll help you." Shade offered his hand.

She eyed it with skepticism before nodding and accepting the offer.

The High Priest raised his hands toward the alastor, chanting in an ancient tongue. I recognized the incantation immediately.

"He is trying to gain control of the demon. You must stop him before the spell takes hold."

"With pleasure." Ember's fingers tightened around the dagger, and the ball of menace I tucked away in my psyche threatened to explode. She could pierce his heart, gut him and take his liver and a prize, making the coven believe a fae had killed him.

I forced my malice into its place, allowing Ember full control. She hurled the dagger, but instead of piercing Adrian's chest, the handle hit his head, making him stumble.

"You missed."

"No, I didn't." She planted her boot into his stomach, and he doubled over. Her uppercut to his chin knocked him off his feet.

The magical tornado ceased its spin, and the alastor dropped to the ground, landing on his feet and rushing her. My goddess spun, jabbing her dagger into the demon's abdomen right where I told her to and twisting the blade with an upward motion.

The alastor wheezed, his eyes bulging a moment before he turned to mist. The rift sucked his essence into the Underworld, and Ember stomped toward the fae. Ash arched a brow as she approached, but she held her tongue, saving her berating words for another time.

My witch straddled the fae, lifting an armored plate and thrusting her blade beneath it, piercing her enemy's heart and draining his life force.

She straightened and turned to the High Priest. "That's Salem five, Boston zero. Who's the real witch now?"

Adrian rose, clutching his stomach with one hand, his chin with the other. "Brute force doesn't make you a witch."

She shrugged one shoulder dismissively. "Maybe not, but it does vanquish demons and kill fae. Do you want our help or not?"

His expression tightened, his gaze dropping to the ground before he met her eyes. "I suppose we can share information, but then you'll return to Salem and let us protect *our* city."

Ember spread her arms. "That's all we want to do. Now, let's shove the dead Bugman through the rift and seal it before any more beasties get loose."

My brother could have easily lifted the fae himself, but he kept up the pretense and merely assisted Ember and the others. Miles took one leg, Ember the other, and Adrian helped Chaos with our enemy's shoulders.

They shoved the body through, and Ash assisted Olga with the mending spell. The veil closed, and Shade and Gray dropped the shadow, bringing the rest of the world into full color. Ember sheathed her weapon, and we walked four blocks to the coven head-quarters.

"I'm going to head home and rest if that's okay," the witch to whom Ash had delivered the antidote said.

"Sleep it off and get ready to fight," Adrian said. "We need all hands on deck."

The injured witch turned down a side street as a three-story, brick building with Boston Society of Magic engraved in the marble above the door came into view.

"I will never get used to witches making their presence known on purpose."

"Times have changed," Ember said before clamping her mouth shut.

"They certainly have, or I would not be inviting you into our coven house." Adrian pushed the door open, and we stepped into a small gift shop filled with trinkets, crystals, and bundles of sage.

The High Priest rested his hand against the jamb of another door and whispered a spell, deactivating whatever ward he'd placed on the threshold. "Our meeting room is this way."

We entered the room, and Ember's mouth tightened as she cut her gaze toward Ash and Chaos. Ash pressed her lips into a thin line, and my brother nodded. They had been here before, and judging by their expressions, no one in this dark coven knew.

"Nice digs." Ember rested her hands on the back of a chair.

A long, rectangular table with at least fifteen chairs crowded around it took up most of the space. At the head of the table sat an ornate throne with dark magic carvings and gilded edges. Olga pulled out the throne, and Adrian sank into it.

"Take a seat." He gestured to the plain wooden chairs. "Tell me what you know about the fae."

Ember mouthed the word *library* to Ash before settling into a chair. Miles and Shade flanked her, and Olga and Gray sat across from them.

Ash remained standing, drumming her fingers on the back of her chair. "I'm the coven librarian, and our library is in shambles. Would it be possible for me to take a look at yours to get some organization ideas?"

"I can take you down." Olga rose to her feet. "We haven't finished cleaning up since the break-in, but I'm happy to show you around."

Adrian cut her a steely gaze, and she shrank in on herself. "If that's okay with you, Priest."

"She did save Hector, sir." Gray's shoulders inched toward her ears, her body drifting slightly away from their Priest.

He straightened his spine. "Give Olga the recipe for your venom antidote, and you may look at the library. But do not open any books."

"Got it." Ash turned to Chaos. "Want to come with?"

"Of course." They followed Olga down the stairs.

"He commands them through fear, but he has not earned their respect." I contemplated this as Ember folded her hands on the table. It was no wonder so many had defected when Chrys offered to overthrow their leadership. The witches in Salem respected the Holland women and did their bidding out of loyalty to the coven rather than fear of punishment.

Interesting...

"We've encountered three types of fae," Ember said. "The blood-sucking mosquitoes, which I'm sure you've been familiar with for years."

Adrian steepled his fingers. "Yes, they always become bothersome this time of year."

Ember leaned back, crossing her legs beneath the table. "The other two are scouts and soldiers. Their exoskeletons are the strongest armor we've ever encountered. They're impervious to fire, but it still hurts like hell when you burn them. Or I assume it does because they screech like banshees when we try."

"They deflect our air witch electricity as well," he said.

"The only way to kill them is to pierce their hearts or behead them."

Adrian blew a hard breath through his nose. "And how, pray tell, do you do that?"

"They have soft spots here." Ember touched the delicate skin beneath her ear. "And their armor is like scales. Get close enough, and you can get beneath them to stab the heart." She sat up straighter. "That's what we know. Your turn."

Adrian studied her, his eyes calculating.

"You might have to force the information out of him. Shall I turn Gray against him?"

Ember cleared her throat, a subtle reminder that she couldn't speak to me. I acquiesced, allowing her to continue the conversation in her own manner.

"I showed you mine. Now, show me yours. What else do you know?" She arched a brow.

He nodded, his expression one of resolve. "Their

leader has contacted me. He is a prince whose name is Ignacus, and he is planning a coup to overthrow his brother and take the crown."

"That's not the story Miles's friend told."

Ember blinked, silently urging him to continue.

"Since I recently experienced and extinguished a coup—led by one of your witches, I might add—I agreed to help him." His lips screwed to the side, his gaze cutting left before he continued. "In return, he promised me incomparable power. I would be the strongest witch ever to walk the earth. I'm sure you can understand the appeal..."

Ember shrugged. "Not really. I'm happy with what I've got."

He chuckled, his disbelief evident in his condescending expression. "But the fae being the fae, he betrayed me. His soldiers have been picking off my team one by one, absorbing their power as they consume their hearts."

"Hearts?" Shade's brow furrowed. "I've only heard about them eating livers."

"The livers provide the enzyme they need to survive in this realm. They eat the hearts of witches to gain their abilities while the scouts search the earth for an amulet that gives its bearer immeasurable strength."

Ember stiffened inwardly, though she maintained her composure. "Do you know where the amulet is? Can we stop them from getting their hands on it?"

"If I knew where it was, don't you think I'd be using it? I'd have sent the overgrown bugs home and strengthened the veil a long time ago."

She leaned back in her chair, her posture relaxing. "Is your team searching for it?"

"Every second of every day since Ignacus told me about it. Your witch Chrys had a piece of it. She wouldn't have had the strength to make so many of my witches turn without it."

Ember tapped her index finger on the table. "So you ransacked her apartment looking for it."

He pursed his lips, shaking his head. "My team searched for it there, but the damage and the murder were courtesy of the fae who followed them."

"Ask him—"

"What's your plan now?" Ember asked, as if reading my mind.

If I had a heart in this form, it would have warmed. Not only was she a skilled warrior, but she was a master interrogator. Her withdrawing this much information without violence astonished and captivated me. I could not wait to have my own body so I could ravish hers.

Adrian steepled his fingers once more. "Find the amulet, murder Ignacus, strengthen the veil, and rule the world."

Ember laughed dryly. "I figured as much."

Footsteps sounded on the stairs, and Ash entered the room, followed by Chaos and Olga. Ash nodded, her eyes conveying conspiracy.

Ember rose to her feet, the wooden chair scraping across the floor with a screech. "Well, thanks for the info swap. We'll get out of your hair."

Adrian rose too, but Olga pulled out his chair, lifting it so it didn't make a sound. "You didn't tell me your plan."

"It's the same as yours, minus the murder and world domination." Ember jerked her head toward the exit, and her team followed.

"It's a race then." Adrian remained in place, not offering the courtesy of walking his guests to the door. "Whoever finds the amulet first wins. I'd wish you luck, but I don't dare put that energy into the ether."

Ember laughed dryly. "Later, loser." She waved and walked out the door.

No one spoke until we reached the end of the fourth block, where Ember paused at the crosswalk and turned to Ash. "Tell me you found the spell."

She patted her pocket containing her phone. "Easy peasy. And Chaos scrambled Olga's mind just enough that she doesn't remember us doing it."

Relief flooded Ember's system. "I love my team."

Ash crossed her arms. "It sure didn't seem that way earlier."

CHAPTER 8
EMBER

"You can berate me later. Let me see the spell." I held out my hand, and Ash's jaw ticked. "You can text it to me if you want, but I'd rather you not send a spell punishable by death through the cloud."

She slammed the phone into my hand.

"Your sister is angry with you."

"No shit." I tossed Shade the keys and climbed into the passenger seat. My team loaded up, and I studied the pictures Ash had taken of the phoenix spell. "Wolfsbane, hyssop...ground bone. Tell me we don't have to sacrifice an animal to pull this off."

"A life for a life. It sounds reasonable."

"Look at the second photo," Ash said. "We need demon bones."

I swiped to the next picture. "'Bones must be of the

same or adjacent species you wish to resurrect.' Fabulous. How are we supposed to harvest bones when demons go poof the second we vanquish them?"

"We'll have to keep one alive." Shade started the van and pulled onto the road. "Put it in a containment circle and harvest a limb before we send it back to Hell."

I cringed. "That sounds barbaric."

"You could exorcize me. I'll possess Adrian and burn through him, solving two problems at once."

"Absolutely not. I already told you that's not an option. You've got enough ego on your own; you don't need to absorb his too."

"Let me guess," Chaos said. "He's suggesting he take the High Priest as a host."

"Bingo. But it's not going to happen."

"It's not the worst idea," Ash said. "If we could take over BSM, we could exile the dark witches and stop looking over our shoulders every time we leave the house."

Surely my sweet little sister didn't mean that. I twisted in my seat to see her face, but she looked as serious as could be.

"That's a hard no." I flashed her a WTF look. "We only kill in self-defense, and even then...only if it's absolutely necessary."

"I can arrange for your self-defense to be necessary. Let's return to Boston, and I'll—"

"Stop it. Both of you. We'll do it like Shade suggested, unless…" I drummed my fingers on my knee. "Chaos, can you regenerate limbs? Maybe if we cut off your finger…"

"Only when I return to Hell." He rested his hand on Ash's thigh. "But I will do whatever it takes to save her."

"Notice his only concern is her. He'd allow me to rot in prison for eternity if her life wasn't on the line."

I rolled my eyes. "It's one finger. I'm sure he'd do it just for you."

"He would not."

"Chaos, would you give up your left pinkie to keep Mayhem out of the dark prison, even if Ash wasn't in danger?"

He missed a beat…two…three. "I believe I would. He has suffered long enough."

"There. See? Your brother loves you." I handed the phone to Ash. "Next steps… How much time do I have with you in my mind? Can we sleep tonight and get started tomorrow without you taking over?"

"Yes, I believe so."

"Good. We all go home and rest. In the morning, Chaos will cut off a finger, and Ash and I will perform the phoenix and exorcism spells. I want you guys to scry for the rest of the amulet while we do our thing, but don't try to retrieve it without us. Understood?"

"Got it," Miles said.

Shade shifted in his seat. "We can help you with the spells. The more power we put into them, the better."

"Not a chance," I said. "I don't want you anywhere near the phoenix. If the Higher Power somehow finds out we performed it, we could be executed. I won't put you in that position."

He blew a hard breath through his nose. "We'll be putting ourselves in that position. It's our choice to help our friends."

"And it's my choice as your High Priestess to say hell no. You're scrying. We're breaking the laws of witchcraft. Got it?"

His mouth pinched, and he gave me the side eye before focusing on the road. "Yeah."

We parked behind the building, and Shade went with Miles to his place. I kicked off my boots the moment we stepped through the upstairs door and set them against the wall before grabbing a can of sparkling water from the fridge and gulping it down.

"We need to talk." Ash sank onto a stool at the counter.

Chaos rested a hand on her shoulder. "I'm going to shower." He kissed the top of her head and strode out of the kitchen, leaving me alone to face my sister's wrath.

"What did I do wrong this time?" I tossed the empty can into the recycle bin.

"Absolutely nothing."

Okay, not completely alone. "I think so too, but Ash disagrees." I leaned against the counter and crossed my arms.

She folded her hands in front of her. "Your ego put everyone in danger today."

I raised my brows. "*My* ego? Adrian's the one who tried to stop me from vanquishing the alastor demon just so he could prove a point."

"And you weren't trying to prove one?" She tilted her head in the same condescending way Mom would whenever I acted out.

My nails dug into my biceps. "He insulted me. He said I wasn't a real witch, so yeah, I had to prove him wrong. You'd have done the same."

"No, Em. You didn't *have* to prove anything." She straightened, crossing her arms. "But you insisted on killing them both by yourself just so you could outshine a dark witch whose opinion doesn't matter."

"But he..." I ground my teeth. "He challenged my authority...my abilities. I had to... And Mayhem was—"

"No." She leaned her forearms on the counter. "Don't even try to blame him. I've seen how his magic affects you, and you acted the opposite. Your behavior today was all you, and it was not okay."

"Don't listen to her. Adrian challenged you, and you had to prove you weren't a coward."

"We are a team," she said, "and you alienated us when you told Shade not to kill the fae. How do you expect the witches of this coven to respect you when you act like that? You stooped to Adrian's level, and it was ugly, Em. So ugly."

"I..." The defensive tension drawing my shoulders toward my ears relaxed, and I let out a slow breath. She was right. I'd gotten so caught up trying to put the asshole in his place that I'd cast my team aside. And for what? To prove myself to a narcissist? I knew better.

I nodded, closing my eyes against the pressure building behind them. "I'm sorry."

"For what? You did nothing wrong."

"Yeah, I did. I put myself...my ego...first. I did the one thing that annoys me the most in other people. I acted alone when I should have depended on my team."

"You lost track of the mission."

"I did, and I'm sorry. It won't happen again." I laughed. "I'm not used to getting called out on my bullshit by anyone other than Mom. Why haven't you done it more often?"

Ash shrugged and traced her finger on the counter. "With my defective magic, I always felt like the outsider. I idolized you for your bravery and fighting skills, but I never thought we had much in common. I guess we never sat down and had a real conversation."

My throat thickened, my fight-or-flight instinct begging me to walk away before I showed vulnerability, but I fought it. This could be a moment for us if I could get out of my own way and let it happen.

"I guess I don't have real conversations with anyone. Showing emotion in battle can get you killed, and... I don't know what's wrong with me." The pressure in my eyes threatened to come out in liquid form.

"There's nothing wrong with you. Everyone's brains are wired differently."

"Absolutely nothing is wrong with you. You are a goddess."

I laughed, and a tear slid down my cheek. "I've always been envious of your relationship with Cinder. I've secretly wanted to be your confidant since you learned how to talk. But I was the one who needed to learn. I just... Goddess, I don't know. What good are words when I can't even string them together in the right order?"

Her brow furrowed, her eyes holding sympathy. "Cinder has always been easy to talk to, so I confided in her out of habit. I'm sorry I didn't try very hard to talk to you."

"You shouldn't have had to." Another tear fell, and I wiped it away. "I'm so sorry, Ash. I'm sorry for never being there for you. For never truly listening."

She rose and wrapped her arms around me. "You're here now. That's what counts."

I sniffled and held her tight. "Yeah. I'm here, and I'm not going anywhere. I love you, Ash."

She pulled away, her eyes glistening with unshed tears. "I love you too."

"We're going to get through this. Whatever it takes, I am...*we* are...going to end this curse and set everything right again."

"Or die trying." She smiled sadly and inhaled a shaky breath. "See you in the morning?"

I nodded and wiped the moisture from my cheeks. "Good night, Em."

"Night." I stayed in the kitchen and watched her walk away. When she disappeared into her bedroom, I double-checked the wards and turned off the lights before heading to mine.

I showered and put on my pajamas in silence. My chest was still tight, my throat thick from our conversation, but the rest of me felt lighter, like a weight had been lifted from my soul. I snuggled into bed, lying on my side and pulling the blankets up to my chin.

"You've been awfully quiet," I said.

"What would you like me to say?"

"Anything. You just witnessed the deepest conversation I've had in my entire life. Don't you have a snide remark about me showing weakness?"

He remained silent for so long, I almost fell asleep. *"Your discussion moved me. Your emotions were familiar yet foreign at the same time, and I don't believe you showed any weakness at all. I found your confession brave and inspiring."*

A smile tugged at my lips. "You think?"

"The more I get to know you, the more convinced I am that we are destined for each other. You make me feel... whole."

"Well, you make me feel like a crazy person talking to herself." I clamped my mouth shut. I'd had a sister bonding moment with Ash, and that was enough feelings talk for one day. Because I honestly had no idea how I felt about Mayhem.

Okay, that was a lie. I did know how I felt...or how I was beginning to feel...and I wasn't anywhere near ready to unpack all that. Hecate, have mercy.

"Goodnight, Your Royal Pain In My Assness."

His chuckle reverberated in my soul. *"Good night, sweet witch."*

I SLEPT BLISSFULLY DREAM-FREE, letting my subconscious process the day so my conscious mind didn't have to. I might not have woken until the afternoon if the sound of shattering glass hadn't yanked me into the land of the living.

I sat up and peered out the window at the back alley, where an imp was using my van as a trampoline. "Oh, for Satan's sake. Chaos!"

I marched out of my bedroom to find Ash and her

demon having breakfast. "Come outside and get your minion under control so I can vanquish him. The effing little bugger shattered my windshield."

I grabbed a butcher knife from the block and rushed down the stairs, not bothering with a jacket or shoes. Chaos and Ash followed, and when we exited the building, the imp yanked off a windshield wiper, gnawing on it like it was a chew toy.

Tiny pebbles in the pavement cut into my bare feet as I paced toward the van, and my arm hairs stood on end as if they could shield me from the cold.

"Stop," Chaos said, and the bastard dropped the wiper to stand at attention for his master.

"Where's the rift?" I adjusted my grip on the knife.

"I don't sense one close by. He must have come through in another area and found his way here, attracted to our auras."

"Good. That means I can vanquish the destructive dickwad." I lifted the knife like Norman Bates, ready to go *Psycho* on the slimy sucker when Ash stumbled.

"Ow! Crap. I stepped on glass."

Chaos, ever the protective boyfriend, diverted his full attention to my sister's bloody foot, losing control of his minion.

The imp took a flying leap at my face.

CHAPTER 9
EMBER

"Son of a basilisk!" I shouted, but I immediately regretted it. Imp slime oozed into my mouth as the bugger clung to my hair, its abdomen sliding across my face and coating my skin in goo.

It tasted like sour milk and disgust.

A tiny worm-like appendage flopped against my lips, and I tried my best to purge my mind of the fact that a gremlin's wee-wee had just touched my mouth. So gross.

I pried the bastard from my face, but it wiggled and slipped from my grip, landing on the pavement with a splat. It was either dazed from the impact or Chaos had regained control, because it lay there in a puddle of slime, its eyes circling as if it were watching something spin.

I hurled the knife at it, but my makeshift weapon

wasn't weighted properly. I missed the bugger's heart, slicing into its shoulder instead. The imp wailed and writhed, the blade pinning it to the pavement as it thrashed.

"Are you okay, Ash?" I called over my shoulder as I marched toward the bastard, scanning the ground for more shards of glass on my way.

"I'm fine."

"Good. Chaos, will you hold this monkey still so I can vanquish it?" I yanked the knife from its shoulder and adjusted my grip, ready to stab it in the heart, but the blade had severed its arm. An idea began to form in my mind.

Under Chaos's control, the imp couldn't wail, but it let out a pitiful, muffled moan through its closed lips.

"Put it out of its misery." Ash hobbled toward me, putting her weight on the heel of her injured foot.

"Wait." I lowered the knife. "We can use it."

"Use it for what?" Ash clung to her demon's arm for balance.

"For its bones," Mayhem said, as if he'd read my mind.

"Exactly." I used two fingers to pick up the severed arm, and the hand contracted into a fist. "The phoenix spell said the bone dust has to be from the same *or adjacent* species."

Ash gasped. "An imp is a type of demon."

I turned toward her, holding up the arm. "And we already have a piece of it."

"You are as brilliant as you are brave."

The imp moaned, saving me from the flutter threatening to form in my stomach.

"If I vanquish it, will its arm go too?"

"Hold it tightly with the intent to keep it...like you did my head...and it will become your trophy."

"If you—" Chaos started, but I clutched the whole arm in my fist, spun to the imp, and plunged the knife into its chest.

With one final screech, the imp turned into a puff of smoke, and a tiny rift opened, sucking it through before slamming shut. As I opened my palm, hellfire erupted on the severed arm, burning the flesh and goo and leaving only bone behind.

"Looks like we just saved your finger. You're welcome." I tiptoed back to the house and wiped the grime from my feet onto the doormat before grabbing the box o' burnt skull and heading upstairs.

Chaos scooped Ash into a cradle carry and followed me, setting her on a stool while I dumped the dirty knife in the sink.

"Let me wash the slime off, and then we'll commit what I hope is the biggest magical crime we will ever have to pull off." I headed for the hall.

"Don't forget about the time spell if we make it

long enough to mend the veil." Ash winced as Chaos picked a piece of glass from her foot.

"One step at a time." I lifted the box, reminding her we had other things to worry about right now.

"And don't forget..." She pressed her lips into a line and cut her gaze toward her demon. "Never mind."

I strode to my room and set the box and the bones on my dresser before gathering a set of clothes and padding to the bathroom.

"You aren't curious what else she wanted to remind you of?"

"Nope." I stripped out of my jammies and turned on the shower. "One thing at a time."

I turned toward the mirror and grimaced at my reflection. Purple hair coated in slime stuck to my forehead, and some strands stood straight up, while the rest was matted into a knot.

"I'm a mess."

"A hot one."

"Haha." I stepped under the stream and closed the curtain before scrubbing every inch of my body and face and rinsing with water as hot as it would go. Mayhem stayed silent while I dried off and got dressed, and I ran a brush through my hair, studying my reddened skin to make sure I'd gotten all the goo off.

"You're awfully quiet up there." I tapped my temple.

"I'm simply going along for the ride."

"Well, fasten your seatbelt and keep your arms and legs inside at all times."

"I don't understand the reference."

"I'm about to commit a magical felony. Don't make me any more nervous than I already am." My stomach soured as I paced down the hall, and when I got to the kitchen, I found Ash gathering the ingredients for the phoenix spell.

The spell I refused to let her take part in.

"Chaos offered to grind the bone so it won't ruin our food processor." She gestured to a stone mortar and pestle.

"Imps are surprisingly sturdy for their size." Chaos sat at the counter and held his hand toward me.

I laid the arm bones in his palm and held his gaze. "I'm casting this spell alone."

"We'll have to source more wolfsbane after this. I never dreamed we'd use this much in... Alone? Why? We can share our vim to—"

"And share a cell when the Higher Power puts us on trial?" I grabbed the mixing bowl from the cabinet and picked up Ash's phone. "No."

"We're not going to get caught, and even if we did...it's for the greater good. We can't save Salem without casting this spell." She started to measure the hyssop, but I took the jar from her hands.

"Try explaining that to the Higher Power. You

wouldn't make it past the 'I accidentally possessed myself with a demon' part." I added two tablespoons to the bowl.

Ash crossed her arms. "I'm the reason we're in this situation. I'm helping."

I scraped the last of the wolfsbane into the bowl, hoping to Hecate it would be enough. "Actually, this guy and this guy..." I jutted a thumb at Chaos and then tapped my temple. "And the one gallivanting through the Underworld with Cinder are the reason we're in this situation, and you..."

"And I what?" She rinsed the empty container and returned it to the cupboard.

I squinted at the screen. "Rose of Jericho? Do we have that?"

"And I what?" Ash took a cedar box from the shelf and handed me a ball of what looked like dried fern.

I broke off a few pieces and crumbled them into the bowl while Chaos finished crunching the bones. Ash's mouth tightened when I tried to hand the herb ball back to her, a vein in her forehead beginning to bulge.

I huffed. "You're already showing signs of the curse. The last thing we need is for dark magic to push you harder into bringing it to life."

Her mouth dropped open, and she took the ball, returning it to the box. "I am not."

I added mustard seed and poured garlic oil on top

of the herbs. "You said yourself that your thoughts aren't very light-witch-like lately."

"Well, I—"

"And you nearly choked on the sage when we tried to contact Hecate."

"It was a fresh smudge stick." She put the box down and crossed her arms. "The smell was strong."

"Ember is right." Chaos slid the mortar toward me. "If she does get caught, she will need you to rescue her before the execution. If you are both detained, your chances of breaking the curse and saving Salem are nil."

She fisted her hands on her hips, her gaze cutting between Chaos and me. "The curse is *not* affecting me yet, but I do see your other point. I don't like it, but I see it."

She tapped a finger to her lips. "I'll cast a magic-containment spell over the room, you cast the phoenix, and I'll conduct the exorcism."

"See? We're still a team." I shoved Ash's phone into my pocket, added the crushed bone to the bowl, and carried everything to my bedroom.

"Why are you doing it in here?" Ash asked from the doorway.

"To keep you out of trouble. If I get caught, you had no idea what I was up to." I grabbed a dagger from my nightstand and settled cross-legged on the floor, setting the items in front of me. "Do your thing so I can do mine."

"Let me go mix the potion." She hurried back to the kitchen.

"You are being *really* quiet. Everything okay?"

"For centuries I have believed witches to be the vilest creatures to walk the earth, but you... You have so many layers. I have to rethink everything I've ever believed."

I laughed. "That's me. Layers for days, just like an onion. Careful or I'll make you cry."

Ash returned with a blue plastic spray bottle filled with an amber liquid. "Are you ready?"

"Absolutely." My stomach clenched and my heart attempted to leap out through my mouth, but yeah. I was ready to get on with the shit show.

Ash sprayed the potion over the walls, floor, and ceiling, giving the doorway a few extra squirts on her way out before reciting the magic-containment spell.

The energy in the room thickened, a blanket of magic wrapping around the space. I took a deep breath...two...three...trying to center myself, but my nerves made my hands tremble.

"You can do this."

"I know." My heart pounded against my ribs. Nausea churned in my gut, and when I leaned toward the door to close it, my knee hit the rim of the bowl, tipping it sideways and nearly spilling the contents all over the floor. Sitting upright again, I took another deep breath and lined up the dagger, the box of Mayhem's ashes, the potion, and the phone.

I can do this. I swallowed hard and swiped open the screen, flipping through the photos to find the incantation. "Oil of garlic, eye of newt, hyssop flower, wolfsbane root? Why do I feel like I'm reciting *Macbeth*?"

"Shakespeare offered his soul in exchange for his works surviving the centuries."

"Oh, wow. So now he's what? Simmering in a tar pit for eternity?"

"Worse. He's eternally putting on plays for the denizens of the Underworld."

"Focus, Ember," Ash called from outside the door.

"Okay." Easy for her to say. She wasn't the one about to commit a magical felony.

I shook out my hands and recited the incantation for real. "Oil of garlic, eye of newt, hyssop flower, wolfsbane root. Like the phoenix, ashes rise. Come back to life before my eyes."

Heat built in the core of my being, mixing and churning with the nausea already permeating my innards. I picked up the dagger and pressed the tip of the blade to my finger. Three drops of blood trickled into the bowl, and the mixture sizzled, turning into a blackened goop before popping and going up in smoke.

"Oh crap." I fanned the fumes into the box of ashes. "I guess this isn't one you can premix and carry with you."

"Everything okay?" Ash asked from the hallway.

"We're good." The smoke sank onto Mayhem's cremated remains, clinging to them like an early morning fog on the dew. The heat in my belly intensified, spreading through my body like a surge of lava from an erupting volcano, and I pushed the magic outward, focusing on the skull.

"Whoa." A rush of adrenaline set my nerves ablaze, and every hair on my body stood on end. My breath came out in a huff before I raked in another one, the sensation of dark, primal power raising goosebumps on my flesh.

The energy kept building and building, and it was all I could do not to shout, "More power. Absolute power!" like Jafar when he's turning into a genie in *Aladdin*.

Holy Hecate.

"Mmm... It feels good, doesn't it?"

So. Effing. Good.

With a final push, I released the magic from my being, allowing every bit of it to encompass Mayhem's remains. The smoke thickened and swirled, and green fire erupted in the box, burning through the cardboard as if it were kindling.

Sparks flashed. Flames crackled. Bone reassembled.

A bang that nearly burst my eardrums rattled the windows. Searing white light blinded me. My head smacked the floor.

"Ember!" Ash raced into the room and cradled me in her lap. "Are you okay?"

I blinked, my vision returning, and I swallowed the thickness from my throat. "I'm peachy," I rasped. "Did it work?"

"Indeed." Chaos lifted Mayhem's skull. "It is whole once again."

"I knew you could do it. You are a goddess."

"Do the exorcism," I strained to speak.

"First, we need to cleanse you of the darkness. Come on." Ash helped me to my feet and guided me to the kitchen. I stumbled, my knees...hell, my every-thing...weak from the power of the spell.

"Rub this on your hands." She passed me a canister of powdered charcoal, and I did as she instructed. "With the energy of a cleansing rain, darkness fades and light remains."

I wiped two charcoal-coated fingers across both my cheeks and inhaled deeply as the icky, sticky dark magic sensation dissipated from my system, taking most of my vim with it. Pressing a hand to my chest, I heaved three more breaths. "That was intense."

"You were phenomenal. With practice, you could—"

"I'm going to stop you right there. There will be no practice of the dark arts in this coven. I hope to never cast that spell again." I chugged the glass of water Ash offered.

"Wash your hands. You're getting charcoal every-where." She wiped the empty glass with a paper towel before carrying a grimoire to the living room. Chaos set the skull on the coffee table, and I dried my hands before sinking into my favorite chair.

"I'm assuming we don't need a containment circle, right?" She opened the book and flipped to the right page. "If you think we do, we'll need to go to my studio for the supplies."

"We're good." I rolled the stiffness from my neck.

"How do you know I won't kill you all the moment I reform?"

"Well, for one...I have your mark. Kill me, and you'll be vanquished." I scooted to the edge of my seat. "No more hunting fae for you."

His chuckle vibrated in my chest. *"And two?"*

I shrugged one shoulder dismissively. "I just know you won't."

My stomach tightened the moment the words left my lips. Did I just know, or were Ash's words skewing my perception of the demon? We were about to find out.

Ash sank onto the corner of the sofa and rested the grimoire in her lap before taking both my hands. We read the incantation in unison three times before I felt the first tingle. My lungs seized mid-breath, and a *boom* from the deepest part of my being shook the entire room, knocking a picture frame from the wall.

I gasped, my entire body feeling as if I'd swallowed a box of staples, the tiny shards of metal raking through my veins and filleting my insides. I coughed so hard, I nearly lost a lung. Purple smoke poured from my mouth, burning my throat and threatening to turn me inside out.

As the final bits of Mayhem left my system, I rose, backing away from the skull. He circled around it, forming a funnel cloud and lifting it into the air. Ash and Chaos stood across the room, watching Mayhem reform.

"Are you okay?" Ash asked for the umpteenth time.

"I'm good." Anticipation tightened my stomach, making my heart race.

Electricity crackled, filling the room with light. The smoke swirled and spun, wrapping around the skull and turning into flesh and bone. The storm dissipated, and Mayhem in demon form stood before me, menace and desire dancing in his eyes.

"Ember." He reached me in two strides and grabbed my shoulders, lifting me from the ground. My pulse thrummed, a strange mix of fear and want flooding my veins and making heat pool below my navel.

"Mayhem…" Chaos's voice dripped with warning.

"You deal with your witch. I'll take care of mine." As if I weighed nothing, he carried me down the hall and into my room, slamming the door behind us. Setting me down, he held my shoulder with one hand and locked the door with the other.

Returning his attention to me, he let go and morphed into his human form. His *naked* human form. *Woof.*

"Are you okay?" He tucked a lock of hair behind my ear, concern etching lines on his forehead.

"I wish everyone would stop asking me that. My vim is taxed, but I'm fine." My gaze slid down his body, over his defined pecs and chiseled abs and locking on his package…unwrapped and standing at attention. My mouth watered. I pressed my lips together so I wouldn't drool.

"Ember!" Ash pounded on the door. "Are you okay?"

"I'm fine. Everything is fine. We're umm…talking." I blinked, looking into his lavender eyes. "Everything is fine, right?"

"You're sure you're okay?" His gaze dipped to my lips.

"Yes." My head spun a little, but I was certain the naked man standing before me was the reason and *not* the events that had just transpired. In fact, all I could think about in that moment was how badly I wanted to climb him.

"You are coherent enough to make good decisions? To speak up if you don't approve?" He arched a brow.

I furrowed mine. "Yes…"

"Good. Then tell me to stop." He clutched my shoulders and crushed his mouth to mine.

CHAPTER 10
MAYHEM

Her lips felt like velvet, plush and soft as they yielded to the pressure of mine. I expected her to pull away. I half-hoped she would, because I knew with every fiber of my being that, if we saw this through to the end, there would be no going back. Not for me.

Not for her, if I could help it.

She lifted her hands, tentatively brushing her fingertips against my chest. The sensation nearly crumbled me. Her lips parted, welcoming my tongue into the moist heat of her mouth, and if I wasn't immortal, I could have drowned in her essence, died in that moment a happy man.

I broke the kiss, and she gasped. "Tell me to stop. Say you don't want this, and I'll walk away."

She touched her swollen bottom lip, tugging it

down slightly as her gaze wandered over my body before meeting my eyes. "That's the thing." She looked at my cock and swallowed hard. "I don't want you to stop."

Her expression held both disbelief and desire as she returned her touch to my chest and traced her fingers over the contours of my muscles. "I could blame it on stress or fatigue or a million other things, but right now, all I want to do is *you*."

My dick throbbed, another rush of blood hardening it even more. "If you're not of a mind to think this through…"

"I don't want to think. It's not my thing. I listen to my body, and I act…leap first, look later…and I am ready to jump into the deep end." Her tongue slipped out to wet her lips, and she trailed her fingers down my stomach, making it tighten.

"You're certain?" I asked.

She inched her fingers closer to my cock. "Do you want me to change my mind?"

"Gods no." I clutched her hands before they went any lower. "But I do plan to take my time, I haven't been with a woman in over four centuries."

"Lucky me for being your first."

First, last, and only for the rest of my existence, but I didn't dare make that proclamation out loud. Whether she believed it or not, she had a brilliant mind. I saw no need to cloud it with declarations of my devotion.

Not yet.

I tugged her shirt over her head, tossing it aside and taking in her beauty. She wore a black satin bra, and I traced my fingers along the edges, caressing the delicate skin of her breasts and recalling the way it had felt when she washed in the shower.

Having been inside her mind, having felt with her skin, I knew which parts were more sensitive than others. She had experienced no sexual yearning at the time, but I had reveled in the sensations fueling my desire.

She reached behind her back to unclasp her bra and dropped it by her discarded shirt. Taking my hands in hers, she placed them on her breasts and then cupped my face, bringing me forward to meet her mouth.

I kissed her, drinking her in as I massaged her breasts, running my thumbs over her nipples and hardening them like pearls. She unbuttoned her pants, sliding the zipper down before working them over her hips, her mouth never straying from mine.

Kicking them off, she leaned into me, the feel of her bare skin against mine weakening my knees. A growl rumbled from deep within my soul, and I wrapped my arms around her, tangling my tongue with hers.

She clutched the back of my neck, sliding one leg up to my hip before lifting herself from the ground and wrapping them both around my waist, the thin satin of her panties the only thing stopping my cock from plunging inside her.

I clutched her ass, digging my fingers into her flesh and deepening the kiss. She moaned into my mouth and moved against me, the motion making promises of events to come and rendering me incapable of speech.

Ember preferred action to words. I didn't have to tell her how this moment made me feel. I would show her. Again and again, until she begged for mercy.

I clutched her waist and shoved her onto the bed. She gasped with the sudden impact, but as she moved to the center of the mattress, a wicked grin lifted her lips. She shimmied out of her underwear, and mischief danced in her deep brown eyes.

I had seen her body through her eyes, but now, seeing her with my own... I could have stood there soaking in her beauty all day long. Instead, I climbed onto the bed with her, moving on my hands and knees until my mouth met hers once more.

"Mmm..." She wrapped her hand around my cock and stroked it, circling her finger over the sensitive head, and I nearly collapsed on top of her.

I hadn't felt a woman's touch in so long...and yet...

Being there in that moment with my soulmate, it

felt as if it really were my first time. It eclipsed every shred of desire or intimacy I had ever experienced, rendering all other moments meaningless.

I grabbed her wrists and pinned her arms above her head, lest she bring our moment to a premature ending. She would come before I did, even if it took all day.

I nuzzled into her neck, breathing in her sweet citrus scent before gliding my tongue from her shoulder to her ear. She inhaled deeply, and as my teeth caught her lobe, her breath came out in a contented hiss.

Releasing my grip, I slid my hands down her arms and cupped her breasts. Her nipples, still hard from my touch, begged me to taste them. I sucked one into my mouth while pinching the other, and she let out the most erotic moan I had ever witnessed.

I wanted...I *needed*... to pleasure her. To make her forget everyone and everything, if only for a few hours. I kissed my way down her body, every intake of breath, every sound she made pleasing me more than my own release ever could.

Emotion swelled in my heart as I realized the purpose of my entire existence. I was made for this woman. Meant to worship her for eternity. Never had I felt this way about anyone. Nor would I ever again.

Ember was my beginning, my end, and everything in between.

I moved down, caressing her legs, kissing, licking, nipping her inner thighs, down one and up the other before blowing a breath across her sensitive nub.

She let out a breathy, "Mayhem, please," that nearly did me in.

My name on her lips turned my skin to gooseflesh, and I slipped out my tongue, swiping it from her slit to her clit. I couldn't have stopped my moan if I'd tried. "You taste so good."

"More," she whispered. "I need more."

I was happy to oblige. I gently sucked her nub between my lips, teasing it with my tongue as she writhed in pleasure beneath me. A bead of wetness rolled down my cock, and I swiped it with two fingers, moistening them before sliding them inside her. She gasped, her core tightening around them as I licked and sucked her most sensitive spot.

She reached for me, tangling her fingers in my hair as I continued my pursuit. Her scent, her taste, the sounds she made...everything about her called to me... to my soul. The tether that had been trying to form between us since the moment I met her tightened its hold.

I belonged to this witch. I would do anything to make her mine.

I slowed, doing my best to draw out her pleasure, but she arched her back and moved her hips against me.

"Don't stop," she whispered.

"I wouldn't dream of it." I twisted my hand, making a come here motion with my fingers inside her. She moaned, her body tensing as I brought her closer and closer to climax.

"Oh, gods, yes." Her grip on my hair tightened, pulling it at the roots, a pleasurable pain searing my scalp as she called out my name. Her hips bucked, and she released my hair to fist the sheets as she rode wave after wave of her orgasm.

"Mayhem," she panted. "I need you. Right now."

"I will give you everything you need. Always." I rose to my knees. "Do you…"

"Birth control. I'm on it." She clutched my dick and guided it to her folds. "Now."

I rubbed my swollen head against her, sliding it two inches in before pulling out and circling her clit with the tip. She closed her passion-drunk eyes, letting out a slow exhale before pinning me with her fiery gaze.

"Don't make me beg again." She lifted her hips, taking me in farther, and I could no longer hold back.

I plunged inside her, sinking into her velvet vise and pumping my hips three times before I stilled. "Tell me what you want."

Her nails dug into my back. "I want you. I want to make you come."

"You first." I moved, circling and thrusting, her

expressions telling me exactly where she wanted me. Focusing on the spot that brought her the most pleasure, I pumped my hips faster, harder. Her core tightened around me, her nails digging deeper into my back until she cried out, release taking her under once more.

"Gods, Mayhem, you're delicious." She clutched my face and kissed me. "I want to feel you come inside me."

I growled and bit her lower lip. "Ask and you shall receive."

My orgasm coiled in my core and released like a monsoon washing over me, drowning me in everything Ember. Talons erupted from my fingers, and my horns began to protrude from my scalp as the beast inside me rode the wave.

Panting, I lowered myself on top of her, burying my face in the pillow to block my semi-transformation from her view. "I'm sorry."

"Don't be." She slipped her hand into my hair, caressing my horns with her fingers. "I know what you are. I'm not afraid."

A half-sob, half-laugh rolled up from my chest. She *did* know. In the short time we had been together, she'd learned more about me than anyone ever had. I lifted my head to look at her and flexed my fingers, drawing my talons back inside.

"I could snap your neck with a flick of my wrist."

She held my face in her hands. "And I could send you back to prison with a swing of my sword."

"Yet here we are, the most unlikely pair, closer than we ever dreamed."

"I'm not ashamed to admit it was the best sex of my life." She pressed a kiss to my lips and tensed, a shadow crossing her features. "But it can never happen again."

CHAPTER 11

EMBER

The second the words left my lips, my stomach tightened and turned, my very being protesting the hypocrisy of the statement. Yes, it was the best sex of my life, and I did want it to happen again. And again and again.

But it couldn't.

Mayhem rolled off me, taking his warmth and compassion with him. His face fell, a curtain slamming down on the vulnerability he'd shown. "I agree. This was a mistake."

"I didn't say it was a mistake." I pushed to sitting, holding the sheet against my chest.

"I did." He slid out of bed and stood, and my stomach tightened even more as I took in the glorious view. My throat thickened, and a tiny voice from somewhere deep inside screamed at me to fix this. To tell him I didn't mean it and that I wanted him in my bed and my life for the rest of my existence.

Down, girl. Don't get attached.

"I spent time inside your mind, and now my mark on your arm is fabricating false emotions. There is no such thing as soulmates, and I was a fool for entertaining the idea. Where can I find clothing? We have work to do."

"Ash's dresser. Bottom right drawer."

He turned on his heel and strode out of my room, leaving me in bed with my mouth hanging open. I don't know what I expected him to do when I said it couldn't happen again, but I definitely did not anticipate he'd plunge a metaphorical knife into my chest.

"Ouch," I whispered, rubbing the phantom pain.

No, not phantom. That pain was real and raw, and I did not enjoy it in the slightest.

I sat still, listening for his voice, but the house stood silent. Sliding out of bed, I padded to my dresser and gathered a set of clothes before heading to the shower for the second time today. His dark, masculine scent lingered on my skin, and I could almost feel his talons against my back as he'd lost control. I had to wash it all away.

After the shower, I scrubbed my teeth and tongue, trying to vanquish the taste of his lips, but it was no use. My mind had grabbed hold of his essence, not just committing it to memory, but etching it in stone.

"Good goddess, Ember. What have you done?" I asked my reflection before I quietly padded into the living room.

Mayhem sat in my favorite chair, his spine straight, his face stoic. Ash flashed me a curious look, and I gave my head a tiny shake, telling her not to ask. I could see the question in her expression: *Are you okay?*

I'll let you know when I figure that out myself.

She nodded. "The guys scried, and they're on their way."

"They're bringing sandwiches," Chaos said, and my stomach growled on cue.

"Do they know where it is?" I sank into the chair opposite Mayhem and tried to make eye contact. He wouldn't look at me.

"You know Shade." Ash folded one leg beneath her. "If they do, he's going to make damn sure we don't go after it without him."

"That tracks." I drummed my fingers on my knees. "The good news is it sounds like the fae aren't planning to take over our realm. If we want to buy what Adrian was selling."

My phone buzzed on the kitchen counter, and I retrieved it, pressing it to my ear. "Another one?"

Higgins huffed. "Washed up at Cat Cove. No liver."

"What about the heart?" I asked as a knock

sounded on our door. I opened it and stepped aside for Shade and Miles to come inside.

"You never told me about an issue with hearts." The crunching of potato chips sounded through the phone. "Is there anything else you've failed to mention?"

My teeth clicked. "I pass on information as I receive it. We only found out about the hearts yesterday."

"Hmm. I'll check with the ME. What else do I need to know?"

"If the heart was missing, the victim was a witch. Liver only means they were human."

"Get this shit under control." The line went dead before I could muster a snappy comeback, which was just as well. My brain was processing way too much information to maintain my sharp tongue.

By the time I finished the call, Miles had set us up with wrapped hoagies and full glasses of water at the table. I sat at one end, and Mayhem took the other...as far from me as possible...while the others filled in the rest of the space.

After firing off a text to Patrice, asking her to wrangle a team to check out Cat Cove, I unwrapped a cranberry chicken salad sandwich and leveled my gaze on Shade. "Well?"

"It's good to have you back," he said to Mayhem, who gave a curt nod, his expression blank.

"Did you find the rest of the amulet?" I took a giant bite of my sandwich and tried not to moan. Savory chicken and sweet, tart cranberries melded together in a flavor explosion. Yum.

"We think so," Miles said. "It's shrouded, but the spell isn't very strong, and..." He cut his gaze to Shade.

"It's strong enough that BSM hasn't found it yet." Shade inclined his chin. "Only a naturally powerful witch could have sensed it like I did."

Miles cleared his throat.

Shade lifted his hands. "Like *we* did. We shared vim."

"*Where* is it?" I couldn't have hidden the annoyance in my voice if I'd tried, but hey. At least I had something else to think about instead of the demon sitting across from me.

Dammit. He was still on my mind. The sigil on my forearm tingled, and I rubbed it to chase away the sensation.

Mayhem inhaled sharply, his gaze snapping to mine. "Don't do that."

Without a word, I picked up my glass and took a long drink. I wanted to spout off a *my body, my choice speech*, but it seemed the tattoo affected his body too. Instead, I squared my gaze on Shade and arched an irritated brow.

"We sense it at Patrice's house," he said.

"That's why we aren't positive," Miles said. "Why would Patrice have it?"

"And why wouldn't she say something if she did?" Ash asked. "You told her we were looking for it."

"I don't know." A sinking sensation formed in my stomach. "You don't think she and Chrys...?"

Shade laughed. "Patrice? She won't even kill a spider. There's no way she participated in a coup with a crazy person."

"Did she ever hang out with you guys while Chrys was manipulating you?" I swallowed the sour taste from the back of my mouth. "We didn't think Chrys was capable of this either."

Miles cast his gaze to the ceiling, looking thoughtful for a moment. "I don't recall her being around during that time. She's always been solitary."

Ash nodded. "And she's healed us more times than I can count. If she wanted to get rid of us, she'd have let us die."

I took another bite of sandwich, chewed, and swallowed as my brain processed the idea. "You're right. It's ludicrous. You probably sensed the amulet's magic there because Chrys used it to trap her in the basement. We need to scry again."

"Or we could go to her house and ask her." Ash rose and carried her sandwich wrapper to the trash. "No sense in wasting vim if we don't have to."

"Great idea." I stood and tossed my trash in the bin. "Everyone, load up."

Mayhem stayed at the table and crossed his arms. "I will remain here."

My jaw tensed, my grip on my water glass tightening. "Fine."

Ash looked from me to him, and back to me. "We don't need the whole crew. How about you and I go, and the boys can stay here and recharge."

"Recharge?" Shade shot to his feet. "It's barely noon. I'm not taking a nap like a child."

"She means our vim." Miles gathered his and Shade's wrappers and wadded them into a ball. "We had to break through the shroud to figure out where it was. I know that taxed you as much as it did me."

"And someone needs to make sure these two don't misbehave." I looked at Mayhem, expecting a sarcastic quip or at least an eye roll. He gave me nothing.

Shade glanced at Miles and sank into his chair. "Yeah. We can do that."

I started to say a silent thank you to Hecate, but with all the trouble we were having finding the damn amulet, it seemed like she'd abandoned us.

"Come on." Ash took a plastic bag from the pantry, grabbed my jacket, and handed it to me. "I just texted and told her we're stopping by."

I checked the inner lining to be sure my knives were there and slipped it on before grabbing the keys and following her downstairs. When we stepped out the back door, I hit the key fob, unlocking the van.

She stopped and put her hand on mine. "I thought we might walk."

"It's twenty minutes on foot. Five if we drive."

She took the keys from my hand and locked the doors. "It'll give us time to talk."

My slow exhale heated the back of my throat. Talking wasn't my thing. Feelings weren't my thing either, and that was exactly what she wanted me to talk about. I chewed the inside of my cheek and gave her the most insolent side eye I could.

She put the keys in her pocket. "It has to come out or it'll fester and make you crazy."

Something inside my chest pinched, and pressure rolled upward, shrinking my throat and threatening to come out as a sob. *What the actual eff, Em?* I closed my eyes and took a deep breath, willing all my insides back to their normal state. It didn't work.

"We had sex." My voice was a whisper over the lump in my throat.

"That much I knew." She laced her arm through mine and guided me to the sidewalk. "I had to cast a silencing spell on your room to give you privacy." I caught her grin from the corner of my eye.

"Thanks for that." I stared straight ahead as we strolled down the street, arm in arm. "It won't happen again."

She waited a beat for me to elaborate. When I didn't, she asked, "Did he hurt you?"

"No." My answer came quickly. He had done the opposite of hurt me.

"Did he force you?"

"Goddess no. I wanted it as bad as he did." A gust of wind blew my hair in my face, and I tucked it behind my ear. "It was good."

"And that's a problem?" she asked.

I blew out a hard breath, trying to find the words to express how I felt. "Yeah."

"Why?"

"Because." I tugged from her grasp to cross my arms. "I'm running a coven and trying to break a curse so we can mend the veil and stop the fabric of reality from unraveling around us...and I am screwing it up every chance I get. I don't have time for romance."

We reached a crosswalk and waited silently for the little red hand to turn into a green walker. When it did, I started to step into the intersection, but Ash stopped me with a hand on my arm.

"You don't have time, or you don't deserve it?" She tilted her head, compassion drawing her brows together, and the pinch inside my chest turned into a vise.

My lower lip trembled as I opened my mouth and closed it again. It still trembled, so I caught it between my teeth and held her gaze, unable to speak.

She clutched my shoulders. "You do deserve it, and he would worship you if you would let him in."

I tried to laugh, but my sob betrayed me. Tears gathered on my lower lids, and when I attempted to blink them back, they spilled down my cheeks. "This is the second time you've made me cry in as many days."

"It feels good to let it out, doesn't it?" She wiped my cheek with her thumb the same way Mom would do when I'd hurt myself.

Another sob-laugh rolled up from my chest. "Have you always been this smart? You see right through me."

The light turned, the red hand flashing before going steady, and Ash pushed the button again. "I don't see through you. I see *you*."

I swallowed, nodding my head and willing the lump in my throat to loosen. "What do you see?" Because I sure as hell didn't know who I was anymore.

"I see a strong, confident, capable woman, who's also filled with self-doubt."

"I'm confident I can kick anyone's ass who crosses me, but that's about it." I wiped my tears and shook my hands, trying to get myself together.

"You're not a people person, and that's okay. You're a full-scale introvert who craves solitude." She shrugged. "We're all wired differently. It doesn't mean you don't deserve love."

The light changed again, and we crossed the street before hanging a right toward Patrice's house.

"Mayhem does love you, you know," Ash said. "He might not express it in a way you understand, but he does. I can feel it."

"It's only been a few days." I tried to scoff, but my heart wasn't in it. I felt it too, and that scared the bejeezus out of me. "He is *so* not my type."

Ash laughed. "He's your perfect match."

"How? You and Chaos complement each other. You're complete opposites. Mayhem and I..."

"Are exactly alike?"

"Not even close. He's hot-tempered and cocky as eff. He's sarcastic and brooding and doesn't play well with others. He's..." I clamped my mouth shut the second I realized who I'd just described. "Well, shit."

"You need to talk to him."

I huffed, shaking my head because I knew she was right. She was always right.

It didn't mean I had to like it. "One thing at a time."

"Some things need to happen simultaneously."

"Not now." I gestured at Patrice's house in front of us. "Let's go see about the amulet."

CHAPTER 12
EMBER

I wiped my face again, running my fingertips over my lashes lest they betray me by holding on to the evidence of yet another emotional outburst. Patrice was crouched near a flower bed, a pair of garden shears in one hand, a bundle of herbs in the other.

I paused on the sidewalk, touching Ash's shoulder and leaning toward her. "Do your thing and see if you can find it while we're talking to her. I want to know if it's here before I bring it up."

Before Ash could respond, Patrice rose and turned toward us. She gasped, dropping the shears and bending to pick them up, her gaze darting around us. "You startled me."

"Sorry about that." Ash strode up the walk, and I followed.

"Is it just you two?" Patrice leaned to look behind us.

"Don't worry." Ash picked up a piece of rosemary she'd dropped and offered it to her. "We know the guys make you uncomfortable, so we left them at home."

"They don't…" She accepted the fallen herb. "They do, but only because they're demons."

"I get it," I said. "It's hard to trust the royal elite of a species we've been tasked to eradicate."

She let out a breath, her posture relaxing. "They don't belong here."

The sigil on my arm heated, making me thankful for the jacket covering it. "No, they don't." Good goddess, they did not. "But we can't save Salem without them. Can we come in? I'd love an update."

Patrice smiled. "Of course. Tea?"

"I'd love some." Ash took the bundle of herbs from her, and I followed them up the porch steps.

While Patrice busied herself in the kitchen, I gave Ash a questioning look. She shook her head, but I couldn't tell if she meant the amulet wasn't there or if she hadn't tried yet.

"Have a seat." Patrice gestured to the breakfast table before turning on an electric kettle and taking three mugs from a cupboard.

Ash sank onto a wooden chair. "How are things going on your end?"

I took the one next to her. "Is everyone still alive with their hearts intact?"

Patrice froze before slowly turning toward me with a furrowed brow. "We've had a few injuries. Hearts?"

I explained what we'd learned about the fae eating hearts to gain the witches' power. "Has anyone fought one?"

She added tea bags to the mugs and filled them with water. "We've come across a few." She set the cups on the table and sat across from us, clutching hers with both hands. "I'm not supposed to tell you..."

I arched a brow. "Tell me what?"

She sighed, her expression one of shame. "We can't kill them. We've tried, but they're too strong. Now, when we find one, we run away." Her brows drew together as her gaze bounced between Ash and me. "I know we're letting you down, but..."

"It's okay." Ash reached across the table to put her hand on Patrice's. "They're hard for us to kill too. Keeping your distance is the best thing to do, especially now that we know what they're here for."

Patrice pulled from her grasp and dipped the tea bag up and down in her mug. "We can handle the rest. Imps, lesser fae, even a midlevel demon or two."

"I know." I sipped the tea and tried not to cringe. Chamomile was not my favorite. "You're doing great. Spread the word that the new protocol is to contact one of us when you run into a scout or soldier."

I moved my leg beneath the table, hitting my knee against my sister's as a reminder of why we were there.

Ash cleared her throat. "Do you mind if I use your restroom?"

"Not at all." Patrice's smile was warm and genuine, and I was glad we could put her at ease. At least about avoiding the upper fae.

"Did Chrys's mom give you any new information? I don't think she had gone through her things before we found the shard of amulet at her apartment."

"No." She folded her hands on the table. "She blamed you for the break-in. I didn't tell her about Chaos and Mayhem."

"Good. No one else needs to know who they really are. We'll be sending them on their way soon enough." I tried to ignore the stab of pain in my chest and took another sip of flavorless tea. Coffee was so much better.

Ash returned from the bathroom and gave me a tiny nod before returning to her chair. "So this amulet... We have to find the rest of it before we can summon Discord and put an end to all this terror."

"Do you have any idea where it might be?" Patrice lifted her mug with both hands and took a long sip.

"That's the main reason we're here." I rose and carried my half-full mug to the sink to dump it. "I had

Shade and Miles scry for it, and they think it might be in your house."

"Here?" Her face pinched. "Why on earth would it be here?"

"Maybe you have it but don't know what it is?" Ash set her empty mug in the sink. "You've got a lot of stuff in your basement."

"I think I'd know if I had an amulet forged in Hell. I don't practice dark magic. Ever." Patrice padded into the kitchen and rinsed our mugs.

"It could be shrouded. Disguised as something else." But hopefully not as a vibrator like the piece in my bedroom.

She stopped rinsing and turned to me. "If I've had it all along and didn't know, I would feel terrible. But I really don't think it's here. I bet whoever shrouded it put a deflection ward on it too. A spell to make you think it resides somewhere it doesn't."

"Do you mind if we look?" Ash moved toward the pantry door and rested her hand on the knob. "I sense it in the basement."

"Of course." She dried her hands on a dishtowel and stepped into the pantry when Ash opened the door. A shelf hiding the entry stood near the left corner, and she tugged it, swinging it open to reveal a set of stairs. She flipped the light switch and made her way down, pausing at the bottom of the steps.

"I haven't been down here since..." Patrice took a deep breath and kept moving.

To the left lay her work area. Massive bookcases held jars of powders, oils, and who-knew-what else. Bundles of herbs hung from a string stretched across the low ceiling, and the aromas of sage and patchouli greeted my senses, reminding me of a demon I didn't have time to think about.

"What does the amulet look like?" she asked.

"It's a red stone." I made my way to the shelving units and scanned the contents. "Opaque, unassuming."

"My crystals are over here." She opened a cabinet filled with rose quartz, black tourmaline, jade, and every other stone imaginable. Grabbing a translucent crimson one, she offered it to me. "This is red adventurine." She grabbed another one. "And this is garnet."

I accepted the stones, pretending to examine them before handing them back. "The amulet is a different shade."

"In here." Ash turned a corner, disappearing into the unfinished section of the basement.

I followed her inside, but Patrice hung back in the doorway. Who could blame her? She'd nearly died in this room.

Ash rummaged through her bag and pulled out a trowel before lowering to her knees and digging in the back corner. I stood over her, watching as she moved the dirt aside with confident movements.

Six inches below the surface lay the rest of the amulet.

"It's here." I looked over my shoulder at Patrice, and she sucked in a sharp breath, bringing her hands to her mouth.

Ash scooped the amulet shard into the trowel and lifted it, revealing a silver chain attached to the top of the stone. "Chrys must have used it to keep her subdued. The spell on those roots was strong beyond compare." She dropped the necklace into a plastic bag and sealed it before sprinkling a premixed potion on the container.

"Vessel tight, vim bright, hold the magic until the end of our plight," she said. "As I will it, so mote it be."

Patrice sobbed, her knees buckling beneath her as she leaned against the door jamb. "I'm so sorry."

Ash dropped the amulet and the shovel into her bag and rushed to Patrice's side, taking her by the arm and helping her out of the room. "You have no reason to apologize."

"But I remember now," she said as my sister helped her into a chair.

"What do you remember?" I stood in front of her, fighting the urge to cross my arms. Patrice was sensitive, a healer. Demanding answers would only make her...

She dropped her face into her hands and cried.

Ash gave me her infamous *shut the eff up* look and rested a hand on Patrice's shoulder. "Take your time. It was a traumatic experience."

She sniffled and nodded, wiping beneath her nose before lifting her head. "She'd cast a binding spell on me, but not like the one we normally use. It squeezed me like a snake. I thought my bones would be crushed."

Didn't that sound delightful? "I'm so sorry you went through that. I should have known it was Chrys. There were clues."

"Were there?" She sob-laughed. "I didn't notice any."

Ash rubbed her back. "Hindsight is always crystal clear."

Patrice took a deep breath and blew it out hard. "She took me in there, to the dirt floor, and called the roots from the ground to trap me. Then she took off the necklace and used her magic to create a hole where she buried it. As soon as she did, dark magic started seeping into my skin."

"Sounds like Chrys." I paced behind her.

"She told me she'd be back for me and the amulet, and that's the last thing I remember until you got me out." She stood and touched Ash's elbow. "I'm okay. Let's get out of here."

We followed her upstairs to the kitchen. Ash filled a glass with water and offered it to her, and Patrice guzzled half the contents before setting it on the counter.

"What will you do with the amulet?" she asked.

"Put it back together, summon the final demon prince, and break the curse Isabel started four hundred years ago."

She wrung her hands. "Do the demons still plan to take revenge on Isabel's descendants?"

I looked at Ash. Her lips formed a thin line, and her shoulders inched toward her ears. "I think so."

Patrice pressed a hand to her chest. "Goddess help them."

I shrugged. "It's them or our entire coven. Our whole town. Thanks for the tea. We'll let you get back to your gardening." I jerked my head toward the door and strode outside, but Ash didn't follow.

Five minutes passed before she joined me on the sidewalk. "She feels awful."

"I can imagine."

We walked two blocks in glorious silence before the hairs on the back of my neck stood on end. I looked at Ash, and her brow furrowed. We stilled, feeling the energy around us, but I didn't sense any type of threat. The sensation felt earthly. Positive.

"What is that?" I asked.

"I..." She tilted her head. "It's the ether...the veil. It feels different."

I opened my senses, letting the vibration wash over me and through me. "Does it feel...stronger?"

CHAPTER 13
MAYHEM

The women had been gone for over an hour, yet the knife in my heart remained. Chaos had assured us he would know if they ran into trouble, that his connection to Ash spanned any distance. I knew it was true because I felt the same bond with Ember.

The knife twisted at the thought of her name.

We had occupied ourselves with the television, Shade and Miles taking the couch while Chaos and I sat in the chairs. Miles had chosen a program about cooking, where humans created dishes for judges to compare, but I paid it no mind.

I couldn't distract myself, couldn't extract the blade of agony from my heart, for my soulmate had rejected me.

Was I too rough with her? My goal had been to

worship her, body and being, but perhaps my perception had been off. She'd seemed to enjoy my affections, and when my beast demanded release, my horns and talons erupting from my skin, she hadn't flinched.

What in Lucifer's name had I done wrong?

I didn't dare seek my brother's counsel in front of the male witches. The business of my heart was none of theirs, and I didn't doubt Chaos would ridicule me for driving the entire meaning of my existence away.

"What's wrong with him?" Shade jabbed a thumb in my direction.

I growled in return before rising and striding out of the room. Ember's bedsheets still lay in a tangle from our lovemaking. The knife twisted harder, and I seethed.

There had to be another vying for her attention. Someone who had entranced her before she met me, confusing her thoughts to the point she could not see that we were meant to be. That there was no other man for her but me.

Hellfire built in my gut, rising up to my chest and melting the blade of betrayal, using the molten metal to fuel my rage. Ember would not betray me. She wasn't capable. The universe had deemed it so.

My palms tingled. Sparks danced across my fingers, gathering into spheres as I curled my hands, my talons erupting from my fingertips. Her interactions with men were few. Their mundane, balding police chief, with his gruff manners and oversized stomach, would never catch her eye. He would need an artifact to entrance her, and he lacked the intelligence to manage one.

My brother belonged to Ash. Of that there was no question.

That left the two males in the living room.

The fire in my palms raged with my fury. I stormed into the room, my expression wild with wrath. Miles saw me first. His knees shot toward his chest before he launched to his feet, springing behind a chair and gathering energy between his hands.

Shade reacted a moment later, joining Miles behind the chair. "Shit, man. Chill."

"Brother…" Chaos stood in front of me, blocking my path, his voice dripping with warning. "These men have done nothing to you."

I moved to the left, attempting to sidestep him, but he moved with me.

"Which one of you has entranced my soulmate?" I growled. "Who has her under his spell? I will rip off your fingers one by one and feed them to you while I skin you alive."

Chaos put heavy hands against my chest, his eyes glowing red in threat. "Neither of them has hurt her."

"Lies. She would not have rejected me otherwise." I shoved him, but he fisted my shirt in his hands and pinned me against the wall.

"Extinguish your fire before you burn this home to the ground. This is *Ember's* home." He released my shirt and used his forearm to hold me down. "Put it out now."

"What in Hecate's name?" The sound of her voice drew the air from my lungs.

I raked in a breath, a fist of anguish clenching my heart. "I will kill them both for what they've done to my soulmate."

Ember's boots thudded on the wood as she stomped into the room, putting herself between me and the treacherous witches. "No one has done anything to me. What is going on?"

Ash joined her in the middle of the room. "Chaos?"

"Apparently, he blames Shade and Miles for Ember's rejection." He turned his head to me, baring his teeth. "Extinguish and relax."

"Mayhem!" Ember fisted her hands on her hips. "Stop it."

At her command, I drew my hellfire inward, my talons following the flames. Chaos loosened the pressure on my chest, but he did not release me.

Ash touched Miles on the shoulder. "It's okay. He'll listen to her."

The men relaxed their defensive stances, though their bodies remained tense, and Chaos removed his arm to rest a single hand against my chest.

"Take a breath with me." Ember inhaled, her chest

expanding before retracting with her exhale. "Do it." She breathed again, and I followed her command. Once. Twice. Three times we breathed together.

The fury in my chest simmered with her presence, her voice soothing me, calming my racing thoughts until I could think clearly. With clarity came the pain of her rejection, and the knife of agony plunged into my chest once more.

She held my gaze as she strode toward me, lifting a hand at Chaos, silently asking him to release me. He backed two steps away, and she rested her palm on my shoulder. Her touch was gentle, but the weight of it nearly crushed me.

"Take a walk with me." She glided her fingers down my arm to clutch my hand. "Come on," she said when I didn't move, and she tugged, taking a step away.

I could do nothing but follow.

She remained silent as we descended the stairs, not turning to look at me until the late afternoon sun illuminated her purple hair, making it shine like silk. We passed her damaged van and turned right on the sidewalk.

"Where are we going?" I asked, unable to bear her silence any longer.

"Nowhere in particular. Walking helps me gather my thoughts." She released my hand to tuck her hair behind her ear. "What was going on in there?

Because it looked like a jealous rage, and that is *no bueno*."

"Your perceptiveness astonishes me." I fought the urge to reach for her hand again and shoved mine into my pockets instead.

"It wasn't hard to figure out." When I didn't respond, she nodded, pressing her lips into a hard line. "So you thought I was involved with Miles and Shade?"

"If I was certain which one had bewitched you, he would be dead already."

"Okay, see?" She stopped and laid her hand on my shoulder, turning me to face her. "That kind of behavior isn't okay. Just because you think someone hurt me or has me under a spell, it doesn't mean you can kill them."

"I would raze the entire world before I would allow anyone to harm you." I grasped her hands, pulling them to my chest. "I would do anything for you."

She swallowed hard, her mouth opening but then closing again.

"Why did you reject me?" I released her hands, returning mine to my pockets so I wouldn't wrap my arms around her and carry her away.

"I didn't reject you. I..." She lowered her gaze.

"You said we could never be together again." I dipped my head, attempting to catch her gaze.

She inhaled deeply and continued walking. "This is hard for me. Words and emotions aren't my thing."

"Nor were they mine until I met you." I walked beside her, matching her strides. "Did something happen in your past?"

"No." She shook her head, drawing her shoulders upward. "It would be so much easier if I could blame it on some traumatic event, but I can't. It's just how I'm wired. I had the same upbringing as my sisters; there's just something different about me. Something wrong."

"There is nothing wrong with you." I grasped her arm, turning her toward me, but she refused to meet my eyes. "Look at me."

It took her a moment, but she finally met my gaze, her deep brown eyes shimmering with unshed tears.

"Words will forever elude me, but the way I feel about you is undeniable. You, Ember Holland, are the reason for my existence."

She laughed and blinked back her tears. "Words don't elude you. The only problem you have is your hot temper. I don't want you killing anyone over me. Understood?"

I frowned. "Not even the fae? Or an attacking demon?"

"That's different. In battle, you have to. In real life...never. Okay? Especially not because you're jealous." She tilted her head, awaiting my answer.

"I will try my best to remember that."

She laughed again. "Your brother has taught me that's the best I can expect from a demon."

"Is that why you rejected me? Because of what I am?"

"Yes and no." She sighed and continued her stroll. "It's hard for a light witch to accept she's fated to a demon."

"Your sister has no problem with it."

"She struggled, believe me. But Ash is better with people than I am, so you have to be patient with me. I'm scared to death of this." She motioned her finger between us.

"And what is 'this' to you?"

"I don't know. I need time to figure things out, and that's the problem, isn't it? We're running out of time."

A crisp breeze rustled the leaves on the ground, and a pink cloud stretched across the sun, dimming the afternoon light as a trail of white smoke extended from the chimney of a nearby home, filling the air with the aroma of burning maple wood. I inhaled deeply, taking in the moment. There would be more like this. There had to be.

"I have waited an eternity to find you. I will wait a thousand more if that's what you need." And I would do everything within my power to make her understand she belonged to me, as I belonged to her. No matter the cost.

She tilted her head, a sad smile playing on her lips. "Yeah, words definitely do not elude you."

I paused beneath an oak tree. "What shall we do now?"

She stopped and faced me. "We need to head back so you can apologize to Miles and Shade. I promise you, they are more interested in each other than they are in me."

My brow furrowed with my confusion. "They are a couple?"

"Not officially...but learn to read the room." She turned around and motioned for us to return. "And put a lid on your pot o' jealousy. It's been ages since a man has caught my eye, and you've given me tunnel vision."

"Tunnel vision?"

She sighed. "You are the only man I am interested in, okay? I like you. Just don't let it go to your head."

The knife once piercing my chest clattered to the ground, warmth and hope replacing the pain. Ember was mine, whether she could admit it or not, and I would never let another man lay a finger on her. I would be her consort, her protector...her everything... just as she was mine.

"This is weird." She huffed out a half-laugh. "You and I are so much alike."

"Why is that weird?"

"Because we're fighters, not lovers. And here we are, taking a walk and talking about our feelings."

I rubbed my chin, my lips pursing. "Very weird indeed. But, according to your television, love can make you do strange things."

She hid her quick intake of air by clearing her throat. "I'm definitely not ready for that word."

It was simple verbiage to express an overwhelming emotion, but I acquiesced. If it made her uncomfortable, I would not use it until she deemed I could. I would do anything for this feisty witch. *Anything*.

We returned to the lot behind her home, and Ember strode toward her van, clicking her tongue as she examined the damage. The imp had shattered the windshield on the passenger side and caused multiple dents in the hood when it jumped.

"It looks like we got hit with a hailstorm." She reached for the hood but stopped, curling her lip at the slime pooling in the dents. "I can't imagine what it'll cost to get this fixed."

"Can you not barter your services?"

"I'm not sure what I could offer a body shop. My talents are throwing sharp objects and killing other-worldly invaders."

"You can offer your protection in exchange for their services. You could make agreements with the entire town."

This time, her laugh resounded from deep in her

belly, the musical sound a symphony to my soul. "A: Ninety-five percent of the people in Salem are clueless about real magic. And B: We're not the mafia. Hold on..."

She leaned toward the windshield, squinting. "What the hell?"

With her thumb and forefinger, she grasped a small piece of rolled parchment. Imp slime oozed from the page, and she held it away from her body, shaking it, the offending goo splattering to the pavement. "Is this a normal thing for an imp to carry across the veil?"

"It's not normal at all. Imps can't read or write, and they only consume paper when meat isn't available."

"So this was either his lunch or a message from someone in Hell."

CHAPTER 14

EMBER

"Ash, get downstairs," I shouted as I flung the door open and stepped into the kitchen. "And bring paper towels."

I darted down the steps and met Mayhem in the library, where he held the rolled parchment over a trash can, saving our floors from imp slime. A minute later, Ash and Chaos joined us.

"Is everything okay?" She tore off two towels and handed them to me. "I told the guys to stay upstairs in case..."

"It's fine. We talked." I waved a hand dismissively. "Look at this." I held out the paper towels, and Mayhem laid the parchment on them.

"What is that?" Ash peered at the scroll. "Where did you find it?"

"On the van. I think it might be a message from

someone across the veil." I rubbed a towel over the parchment, soaking up the slime.

"And they sent it with an imp?" Her arched brow conveyed her skepticism.

"Remember Miles's friend Wendy saying Adrian sent messages back and forth with the lesser fae? Do you have tweezers?" I sank into the chair at her desk and turned on a lamp.

She opened a drawer and took out a fabric bundle before laying it next to the parchment and unfolding it. A set of silver tools shined in the lamplight, complete with scissors, a scalpel, and three different sizes of tweezers.

I chose the medium pair and a blunt instrument and carefully unrolled the parchment. Ash watched over my shoulder, and Chaos and Mayhem stood across from us, leaning forward to read the elegant script. I recognized the handwriting instantly, and my pulse quickened as I read the letter.

Ash and Ember,

I'm afraid the imp might devour my message before it gets to you, but I have no other way to send it. Halloween will be here before we know it, and the veil has already become too weak to bear its natural thinning. We're doing everything we can to keep it intact, but even the goddess can't hold it forever. There's an amulet somewhere on your side. You have to find it and summon Discord so he can

*return it to its rightful owner. I can't come home
without it.
Blessed be,
Cinder*

ASH LAID her on my shoulder. "She's alive."

I released the parchment, letting it curl into a loose roll, and placed my hand over hers. "And we can bring her home."

"Did you find the amulet's missing piece?" Mayhem asked.

I smiled up at him. "We sure did. Let's go put that baby back together."

I wrapped the parchment in the paper towel and put it in Ash's desk drawer before leading the way upstairs, with Mayhem behind me and Chaos and Ash following. The moment I opened the door, Miles and Shade shot to their feet, their energy teetering between fight and flight.

"Mayhem has something he'd like to say to you before we put the amulet together." I started for my room, pausing at the hallway to listen.

He stayed in the kitchen, a safe distance away from the guys. "I no longer wish to kill you."

I crossed my arms. "That's not an apology."

"Princes of Hell do not apologize." He relaxed his stance. "However, my behavior was fueled by distress and rage, and I should not have acted before speaking with Ember. Please accept my humble apology." He bowed regally, though I couldn't tell if it was sarcastic or sincere.

Miles stepped toward him. "We would never try to come between you and Ember. Fate is fate, and we won't tamper with it."

Shade stepped to his side. "Fate or not, neither of us is interested in her like that. We never have been."

"I know. She informed me of—"

I cleared my throat, stopping him from finishing the sentence. Just because I knew the bond between Miles and Shade, it didn't mean they had figured it out yet.

"Apology accepted." Miles offered his hand, and Mayhem shook it.

"Just don't mess with us again." Shade shook his hand as well.

"I will do my best," Mayhem said.

"And that's the best you'll get from him." I started down the hall but paused, turning back to them. "Are we all good?"

"We're good," Shade said. Miles and Mayhem nodded.

"Good." I strode into my room and retrieved the shard of amulet from my nightstand drawer. When I returned, Ash had set the piece from Patrice's house on the counter. I laid mine next to it.

No one said a word, but they all looked at me like I'd grown horns. "What?" I asked.

"Is that a mechanical penis?" Mayhem's face scrunched with confusion. "It's rather small."

"I cloaked it in case anyone tried to find it. Let me remove the spell." I held my hands over it. "What I've done is now undone. As I will it, so mote it be."

Nothing happened.

Ash pressed her lips together, holding in a laugh. "Em, that's your real vibrator."

"No, it's..." I looked at the object in question, and my cheeks heated. "Shit, it is. Hold on." I snatched it off the counter and speed-walked to my room.

My ears burned as I opened the drawer and traded the real deal for the fake one. I couldn't tell you why I was embarrassed. So what if I used it on the regular? I hadn't had a date in ages, and women had needs too.

But Mayhem had seen it. He'd called it small, which, from his point of view, I supposed it was. But it didn't matter. I had a sexy demon prince ready to worship me if I ever had time to fulfill my womanly needs again.

Oof. Was that a good thing or a bad thing?

"This is it," I said as I returned to the kitchen and laid it on the counter. "What I've done is now undone. As I will it, so mote it be."

The vibrator transformed into the plastic jar with the amulet shard. I opened it, spilling the contents, and Ash did the same with her piece before opening her toolkit and taking out a pair of small wire cutters.

"What did Patrice say about the amulet?" Shade asked. "Where did you find it?"

"It was buried in her basement where Chrys was holding her with the roots." I grasped the tweezers and held the shard still. "She buried it there to keep her spell in place. Patrice had no clue until we jogged her memory."

"Damn," Miles said. "I hope it wasn't there to temper her magic like the ward Chrys put on this building."

"If it was, it's gone now." Ash clipped the cage holding the piece of amulet, bending the wires so I could dump the shard onto the countertop.

"I don't think the chain belongs on this piece either." I gestured to the one we'd retrieved from Patrice, and Ash turned it over. "I guess the original one broke off. It looks like she used glue to attach it."

"Indeed, it does," Mayhem said. "The amulet used to hang from a chain of gold, forged in Hell."

"Do we have to find the missing chain too?" I asked.

Mayhem shook his head. "No, it is the stone that contains the magic. Discord wore it constantly, taunting me with its power."

I snapped my gaze to his. "Don't get any ideas. We're using it to summon your brother so he can return it to the Underworld. Period. Nothing else. Got it?"

"I understand." He held my gaze, and the purple in his irises seemed to undulate in a mesmerizing wave.

A sense of calm washed over me, and for a brief moment, I actually believed everything would be okay. Funny, I know.

I blinked, pulling myself out of the trance and landing firmly in reality. Everything would *not* be okay. The demons had to return to Hell. We had to stay here. Even if we broke the curse, there would be no happily ever afters for us. The thought pained me.

That was why it was best not to get attached. I made a mental note not to forget it, wadded up the emotions, and shoved them into the deepest corner of my mind. With any luck, they'd stay there.

"Ready?" Ash asked.

"As I'll ever be." I used the tweezers to pick up the shard and touched it to the amulet.

We held a collective breath as both pieces of the stone glowed deep red. Heat crept up the metal instrument I held, and while it couldn't burn me, life had taught me heat that intense would melt a mundane's skin. Hell, it would melt a witch's too if fire wasn't her inborn power.

I released the shard and set the tweezers down.

The stone pulsed, and the broken piece moved across its surface, melding with the place it had been broken off. A flash of crimson light filled the room, blinding me for a few seconds.

When my vision returned, I blinked the amulet into focus. The glue holding the makeshift chain had dissolved, but the shard fit perfectly, no cracks or lines revealing it had ever been broken. It was rounded and smooth on the left side, creating one half of an oval.

On the right side...

"Jagged edges." My heart sank. "There's another missing piece."

CHAPTER 15
EMBER

"One thing." I paced across the living room, turned on my heel, and paced back. "Why can't *one* thing be easy?"

"To quote our High Priestess, 'Where's the fun in that?'" Ash dropped the two-thirds-complete amulet into the plastic container.

At least, I hoped it was two-thirds complete. If we were missing any more pieces, I might... Ugh. "I've had all the fun I can handle." I resumed pacing.

Shade sank onto a stool at the counter. "We'll find it. It has to be somewhere in Salem or Boston."

"Does it?" My fists clenched, my nails digging into my palms.

"Could it be buried here?" Miles asked. "Since she put up a ward to temper your magic, maybe she left a piece somewhere outside."

"There's nowhere to bury it," Ash said. "And the spell she used on our house wasn't strong enough to require magic like that."

"And we don't even know if she had all the pieces." The heels of my boots thudded on the hardwood. "Was Chrys the one who broke it, or did Isabel do it? Or one of her descendants? We have to scry again. Halloween is next week."

"I'll set it up." Ash padded to the kitchen and filled a bowl with water. "We should all do it together."

I lit two candles and set them on the table. Ash put the bowl of water between them, and everyone took a seat. I laid my hands on the table, and Ash rested her palm in mine. Mayhem hesitated, his questioning gaze dancing across my face, and I nodded.

The moment his skin touched mine, a jolt of... something...shot straight to my heart. My chest tightened, and for a moment, I forgot to breathe. Apparently, this was what holding hands with your soulmate did to you.

The sensation wasn't unpleasant in the slightest. I'd grown used to the pinpricks skittering across my skin, but now they burrowed deep inside me, making my nerves come alive. He must have felt it too, because a hint of a smile lifted the corners of his mouth as he offered Shade his other hand.

Wariness tightened Shade's features, but he recovered. When everyone had joined hands, I inhaled deeply, centering myself and trying my best not to think about the hot-as-sin demon sitting next to me. *Don't get attached, Em. Don't get attached.*

"Everyone ready?" I asked.

"I don't know how to scry." Mayhem squeezed my hand. Definitely not unpleasant at all.

"You just have to share your energy with us," I said. "We'll focus it into locating the amulet."

"Very well." He opened to me before I was ready, a surge of demon magic coursing through my psyche, making me gasp.

Shade's brow furrowed. "How about a little of that over here?"

Amusement sparkled in Mayhem's eyes as he withdrew a fraction of his magic and offered it to Shade. My stomach looped at his playful expression, so I focused on the water bowl instead. If I didn't get myself under control, this would never work.

"Let's begin." I gazed at the water in the bowl, the candle flames filling the periphery of my vision until everything started to blur. I allowed my sight to remain unfocused and thought about the amulet.

Forged in the depths of the Underworld. A joint project between Hecate, our goddess, and Hades, their god. Why would a god and goddess need an artifact that increased a being's power beyond compare? I couldn't fathom it. Then again, I'd never met a deity. Who knew how their brains worked?

Picturing the red stone in my mind, I held on to the image, visualizing the broken piece and how it would fuse with the rest of the gem. Ash's energy vibrated high on my right while Mayhem's low rumble pulsed on my left.

I invited both into my psyche, letting them mix and meld in the core of my being, pulling me deeper and deeper into the trance. Though my eyes remained open, I saw nothing but the darkness of the ether, which I sifted through as if it were sand running through my fingers. All I felt was the void.

"Does anyone sense it yet?" My mouth felt dry, my tongue sticky.

"Nothing yet." Ash's voice was hoarse and thick, a side effect of the scrying trance. "Let's go deeper."

I inhaled and let out a slow, controlled breath before allowing myself to slip in further. The outside world ceased to exist. I couldn't feel the hands I held nor smell the burning wax. With all my senses focused into the ether, I searched for the energy of the amulet.

A tickle formed in my consciousness, the sensation pulling me forward. "*I feel something,*" I said silently.

"*Share it,*" Ash replied in my mind.

I did, allowing it to seep into our shared trance, and a vision began to form. It wavered, sparkling around the edges and fading in and out. My only thought the matter at hand, I focused harder, bringing the amulet into clear focus.

The sparkles dimmed as the image took shape, an unassuming red stone attached to a shimmering gold chain.

"*That's it, right?*" I asked the demons, but they couldn't reply. Even though they shared their magic with us, they weren't part of the collective trance.

"*It has to be,*" Shade said. "*Pull back so we can see where it is.*"

I pictured the area around the stone. It lay nestled on a pillow of black velvet. Pulling back further, I saw the plexiglass container holding it on a shelf. It sat in a massive storage room, with rows and rows of shelving units. Jewelry, hand-drawn maps, and pottery filled the shelves, and antique furniture lined the floors.

"*What the hell?*" I pulled back more and found security guards armed with assault rifles at the entrance to the room. The vision wavered, the sparkles returning to the edges.

"*Stay in the trance. We need to see where the building is.*" I sent out another wave of magic as I pulled back in the vision. A lobby. Three sets of heavy double doors. More armed guards. Finally, I made it out of the building, a brick and glass structure that stood at least ten stories high.

"*I recognize this,*" Miles said. "*I know where it is.*"

"*Let's pull out, then. We've used enough vim.*" I took a deep breath, bringing my senses back into my body. The candles' blurry flames flickered in my peripheral vision, and warmth from Mayhem's and Ash's hands seeped into my palms. I blinked the water bowl into focus and gasped, letting go of Ash to press my hand to my chest.

Mayhem held my other hand tightly. "Are you okay?"

I looked at him, the concern in his gaze making me feel things I didn't know how to name. "I'm good. Everyone good?"

"Yeah," Shade said, and Ash nodded.

Miles's brow furrowed. "I'm okay, but...someone put the rest of the amulet up for auction. It's in New York City."

"A heavily guarded auction house. Fabulous." I rolled my neck from side to side, stretching the tension from my muscles and hoping my spine would crack to relieve some of the pressure threatening to build into a massive headache. Sadly, it didn't help.

"Human guards will be no match for a Prince of Hell and his fire witch. We will simply go in and take what is rightfully ours."

"Whoa. There are so many things wrong with that sentence." I tugged from his grasp and stood before extinguishing the candles and carrying them to a shelf. A trace tingle of Mayhem's magic still danced across my skin, so I shook my hand, chasing away the sensation.

Mayhem stretched out his legs, clasping his fingers behind his head. "It makes perfect sense to me."

My teeth clicked, the tension in my jaw adding to that in my neck. "Let me dissect it for you. A: We don't know for certain all the guards are human. That's a high-paying job, and witches have to work too. So do shifters for that matter, and New York is home to plenty of them."

He started to respond, so I held up a hand to stop him. Miraculously, he obeyed, though I didn't miss his smirk.

"B: Even if they are all human, I can't stop a bullet, and if I die, you get vanquished. You have to remember that."

He lifted one shoulder dismissively. "I would never let that happen."

"C and D: I'm not *your* fire witch, and however we decide to handle this, we will be working as a team. We *are* a team. No more solo side quests."

Ash nodded her appreciation.

"And F—"

"You're on E," Shade, ever the helpful one, chimed in.

"E is for everyone. F: There won't be anything simple about this. In addition to the armed guards, the building will have cameras and an alarm system to notify the police if anything goes awry. As much as

Higgins is a thorn in my side, he protects us from the law here. He can't do that there."

"So we're screwed." Shade lifted his hands and dropped them in his lap.

Ash took the bowl to the sink and dumped the water. "Not necessarily. We could find out when the auction is and go there to bid on it."

"That's a possibility." I paced the length of the living room. "Miles, do you know the name of the auction house? Can you look it up?"

"Yeah." He swallowed hard, sadness tightening his eyes. "Ginger and I spent a weekend in a hotel nearby. We'd hoped to sit in on an auction, but nothing was planned for when we were there."

Shade's brow crumpled. "I'm sorry."

Mile's face twitched before his expression turned neutral. "It's alright. Let me grab my laptop. Can I use your wifi?"

"Of course."

He rose from the table and took his computer to the living room, setting it on the coffee table before sinking onto the sofa. I recited the password, and after he connected, he pulled up the auction house website.

"I'll have to make an account to see the items up for bid." His fingers flew across the keys.

I sat next to him. "Use a fake name. We don't need anything traced back to us if we have to steal it."

He gave me the side eye. "I work in IT."

"Right." I raised my hands in surrender and let him do his thing.

Mayhem sat in the chair adjacent to my spot on the couch. I could feel his gaze on my face as Miles created a fake account for Boyd Anderson from Houston, Texas. He even used "BigOil" as the email address.

I laughed. "Why do I get the feeling you've done this before?"

Miles cleared his throat. "I'm in."

"You claim to be light witches, yet you are firmly grounded in the gray." Mayhem still watched me.

"It's okay when it's for the greater good." I didn't dare look at him, lest he derail my thoughts all over again.

"The auction is scheduled for tomorrow evening. In person only." Miles clicked the event and opened the page of items that would be up for grabs.

"How long is the drive to New York?" I asked.

Ash typed on her phone. "About four and a half hours without traffic."

"We can manage that." I watched as he scrolled through the items, many of them artifacts we'd seen when we scried. He found the amulet in the list between an eighteenth-century vampire-hunting kit and a gem-encrusted swan figurine and clicked the entry.

"'A genuine nineteen-carat Burma ruby attached to a twenty-inch gold chain of twenty-four karats.

Circa 100AD.' I wonder where they got that information?" I leaned forward, resting my elbows on my knees.

"The amulet is no earthly gemstone," Mayhem scoffed. "It was created in Hell, not in Burma."

"The humans don't know that." I patted his thigh, and he sucked in a quick breath. Jerking my hand back to my lap, I glanced at the others. They either hadn't noticed, or they were choosing to ignore the whatever-it-was going on between me and the demon. *Thank you, Hecate.*

"Bidding starts at $400,000," Miles said.

I blinked before squinting at the screen. "Are you sure that's five zeros?"

He zoomed in so I could see it clearly. Yep. Five zeros. "I don't think bidding is an option. Or...is it?" he asked.

I barked out a laugh. "Maybe if we sold the house, all our weapons, and the library."

"Don't you dare touch my books." Ash's phone buzzed, and she swiped open the screen before letting out a dry chuckle. "Patrice wants to know if we've mended the veil...and if the demons are back in the Underworld."

"I wish." I stood and sidestepped Mayhem to resume my pacing. "I mean...not the demons back in Hell part." I made the mistake of looking into Mayhem's eyes and found fierce determination staring back at me. Why did I get the feeling that returning to the Underworld wasn't on his agenda?

Her phone buzzed again. "She said things have been eerily quiet today. They haven't battled a single beastie."

"It must be Hecate's work. Cinder's letter mentioned they were trying to hold it together from that side." My head spun, the vim depletion from the scrying session finally surfacing above my adrenaline.

"She did mention that even a goddess can't hold it forever," Mayhem said. "Discord must have convinced Hecate to help."

"Or Cinder did." I dug my fingers into the muscles at the base of my skull, massaging the tension. "We have no clue what's happening across the veil right now, but we need to take advantage of the quiet."

Pain ached from my skull, down my neck, and into my shoulders, but I couldn't focus on that right now, because... "We need to plan a heist."

CHAPTER 16

MAYHEM

Ember clutched the back of her neck and paced the length of the living room, back and forth, back and forth, until I would have sworn she'd wear a trench into the wood. The stress of leadership was taking a toll on her body and her mind, and a spark of misplaced anger ignited in my being.

Instinct told me to place blame, take action, and get revenge for the pain my witch endured. But who could I condemn? If her parents had not summoned the trickster that took them to Hell, her sister would not have made a deal with Discord. Ash would not have summoned Chaos, and I would still be rotting in my dark prison, devoid of all my senses, going out of my mind.

Worse than that, I would have never experienced the fierceness of love I felt for my soulmate.

No, I could not blame her family for her pain. The universe planned the chips to fall exactly as they did to bring us together, and now that my brothers and I had found our missing halves, it was up to all of us to ensure we experienced the elusive happily ever after.

Ember stopped pacing, lifted her hands, and dropped them at her sides. "I've got nothing. If it were a magical heist, I'd already have a plan, but we're dealing with humans, guns, and a possible prison sentence, which is one thing we don't have time for."

"I can make them turn their guns on each other. Then we can slip into the vault and take the amulet while they are transfixed in battle."

"Absolutely not." She put her hands on her hips. "No killing humans."

"Technically, they would be killing each other." I rested my elbows on the arms of the chair and steepled my fingers. "You wouldn't have to harm a soul."

She closed her eyes, her nostrils flaring as she blew out a slow breath. This expression, I had learned, was one of annoyance, and Hades forbid I should become an accessory to her pain.

"No killing humans," I said. "Understood. But you must understand if your life is in peril, I will act accordingly to keep you safe. There may be casualties."

"The same is true of me," Chaos said. "Your lives

are worth more than a prison sentence...and no human jail could hold us anyway."

Miles chuckled. "I wish I could find someone who'd protect me with such grit."

"I've got your back," Shade said.

I glanced at Ember, who lifted a brow, her expression conveying what words could not in their presence: *See?*

I gave her a small nod. *Yes, I see.* Hopefully they could find their happily ever after as well.

My brow furrowed. Where had a thought like that come from? As a Prince of Hell, I never cared about...or even considered...the emotions of others, yet the idea that the two men should be happy together rooted firmly in my chest.

How strange.

"Fine." Ember crossed her arms. "But only if it's absolutely necessary to save one of our lives."

"Agreed." I couldn't stop the smile from lifting my lips. Her passion and determination warmed my coal-black heart.

"That sounds reasonable," Chaos said.

"Good." She resumed her pacing. "We'll leave first thing in the morning so we can scope out the place in the daylight. We need to get in, grab the amulet, and get out without causing a scene."

I held in my laugh. She had Chaos and Mayhem on her team...there would always be a scene.

"If you believe the movies," Ash said, "the best time to grab it would be when they're transporting it from the vault to the auction room."

"Yes, that's good." Ember pointed at her sister. "You and Chaos can go in and do your mind control thing. Make the guard hand over the amulet."

Miles had been typing on his laptop, but he stopped abruptly. "There will be at least three guards and an auction official who move it. It's a standard security protocol for high-value items. You'll have to mind control all of them to make it happen."

"Oof. I'm not sure we can do that." Ash rose from the couch to sit on the arm of my brother's chair. "What do you think?"

Chaos rubbed his thumb and finger on his chin. "I can cause chaos to the masses, but your magic is much more focused. I wouldn't chance it without practicing it first."

"You can try it on us," Miles said. "As long as you don't make us do anything embarrassing."

Shade shrugged one shoulder dismissively. "I'm game."

The memory of what happened when I used my power on Ash made my stomach sour. "You will not attempt to control Ember. I will not allow her life to be put at risk."

"Wait. This is deadly?" Shade held up his hands.

"The reason I vanquished him was because he

tried his magic on Ash and it got stuck. Her bond with Chaos did something weird to the connection, and Mayhem couldn't let her go." She stretched out her arm, gesturing to my mark on her skin. "And now I'm bonded with him."

Possessiveness tightened my chest. I wanted to take her, to wrap my arms around her and return to Hell, where could spend eternity together. But it would not be our happily ever after. My witch would never leave her family and her duty to her coven behind, and if Ember wasn't happy, I could never be.

"Try it on them. If you can control two, you can manage four." Ember sat on the arm of my chair and massaged her neck, stretching it from side to side as her fingers dug into the muscles.

Her close proximity set my nerves ablaze. She didn't touch me, but she didn't need to. Our bond electrified my soul.

Chaos took Ash's hand, and they both focused on the men. "Miles, you will give your computer to Shade."

Miles's expression blanked, and he nodded. "Yeah. Here you go." He slid the computer into Shade's lap.

"Shade, you will bring it to me so I can destroy it. Miles, stand up and bring me a beer."

Miles did as he was told, padding to the kitchen and taking a beer from the refrigerator.

Shade laughed and closed the laptop. "I don't think so. This thing cost him two grand."

My brother and his witch exhaled, releasing their hold on Miles. Confusion furrowed his brow, and he looked at the beer in his hand.

"I see it worked on me. Do you still want this?"

Chaos shook his head. "We could not control you both."

Miles put the bottle into the refrigerator and returned to his spot on the sofa. "So that plan won't work." He opened the laptop and typed rapidly.

Ember pushed on a spot in her shoulder and groaned.

"Are you okay?" Ash asked.

She kneaded her muscle. "I've got a knot right here, and it's giving me a headache. I can't think straight."

I held my hand toward her. "May I?"

Her hesitation pierced my heart, but after giving me a wary look, she said, "Sure."

Miles continued typing while Shade watched the computer screen. My brother stared at me intently, and for once, I could not read his expression. If it were one of warning, I couldn't fathom what he'd warn me about. This witch belonged to me. It was my duty to keep her happy, healthy, and pain-free.

I rubbed my thumb against my fingers, gathering heat on my skin before placing my hand on her shoulder. I squeezed the muscle she had indicated was ailing her, and it was as taut as a guitar string. With my thumb, I applied pressure, moving it in slow circles over the tightest spot.

Ember groaned, sliding from the arm of the chair to sit on the floor in front of me. "Keep doing that."

Blood rushed to my groin as the memory of our morning encounter played in my mind's eye. I leaned forward, using both hands to massage the tension from her shoulders.

"How are we going to get close to it if it's that heavily guarded?" she asked. "We could use a binding spell but I'm sure they'll have cameras everywhere. We can't go in wearing ski masks."

"I'm on it," Miles said while typing furiously.

Ember leaned back against the chair, nestling between my legs and pitching her head forward, giving me better access to her neck. My entire being ached to be closer to her. To rid ourselves of our clothes and bask in each other's essence. I would massage her from head to toe until every ounce of tension released from her body.

"What are you doing, Miles?" She rubbed her temples.

"He's hacking into the auction house's network," Shade said.

Ember's head snapped up. "You're a hacker?"

A blush spread across Miles's cheeks as he drew his

shoulders upward. "It started as a hobby, just to see if I could do it."

"Now companies hire him to hack their systems and find the weak spots and back doors." Shade smiled proudly. "He's good at his job."

"I'm alright." He grimaced at the screen. "They need to verify Boyd's funds. This is going to take me a few hours."

"What's the plan?" Ash asked.

Miles closed his laptop. "I need more power than this. I'll have to go home to finish it, but I will have it done and be ready to go in the morning."

"And you can get us in and out without causing a scene?" Ember asked.

"That's what I'm working on. You have to be registered in their system before they let you through the doors. High-dollar clients can view items up close before they head to the auction floor, which means I have to make Boyd a fake bank account for them to verify. It'll take time."

"M'kay." Ember melted into me, her head tipping back. "Go home and set it all up. Miles, you're taking point on this. Let us know what we need to do."

He rose and put the computer into his bag. "Will do. Oh, and Boyd is from Texas, so one of you will have to learn the accent. I recommend watching *Dazed and Confused* to hear what it really sounds like. Particularly listen to the character David Wooderson. Matthew

McConaughey is actually from Texas, so you know it's authentic."

The men left, and Ash spoke into the remote control, "Play *Dazed and Confused*." The television responded, bringing up the movie she requested.

"In the past, they would have called this technology witchcraft." I squeezed Ember's shoulders, making her melt even more.

"They called most things they didn't understand witchcraft." She rested her hand on mine, stilling me. "Thank you. It's okay now."

"I can continue if you need more."

She laced her fingers through mine, sending a jolt to my heart. "I'm good. I am starving though. Pizza?"

"I'll order it." Ash used her phone to request the delivery, and the movie began.

Ember didn't move from her spot on the floor. She continued holding my hand, and I fought the urge to pull her into my lap. She had said she needed time to come to terms with our bond, so I would not push her. We remained in the position for half an hour, watching a movie about teenagers acting like imps in Texas.

When the pizza arrived, Ash paused the movie, and she and Chaos went downstairs to retrieve it. Ember inhaled deeply, sliding from my grasp before rising and heading to the kitchen. I immediately missed the sensation of her body nestled against mine.

She gathered plates and napkins and filled four glasses with water, setting them on the coffee table before pausing and looking at me. "I'm going to move to the couch. My butt's getting sore from the hardwood."

She sat down and moved to the middle seat. When she settled in, she glanced at me and looked at the empty space next to her.

She did not have to ask me twice. I moved from the chair to the couch before she could change her mind, sitting close enough that our knees touched as I turned toward her.

"You are the High Priestess, yet you're allowing Miles to make the decisions about this important quest. Why?"

She shrugged. "I know my limits. My way would be to bust in, knock everyone unconscious, and take it, but I know that's not the best way to do it."

It would have been my first choice as well, though I wasn't sure I could restrain myself enough to simply make the guards unconscious. "It would be efficient."

"Or we could end up in jail...or dead. I trust Miles. If he says he can get us inside without violence, I believe him."

"And that is the sign of a good leader," Ash said as she set the pizza boxes on the counter. "Relying on your team and working with their strengths is the best way to get things done."

Ember laughed. "Yeah, I'm still learning that."

"You're doing great." Ash filled our plates and sat next to Ember before starting the movie again.

We ate the glorious concoction they called pizza as we listened intently to the characters in the movie. The flavors of melted cheese, three different meats, and tomato sauce melded perfectly atop the floppy slices of bread, making my tastebuds rejoice.

When the movie ended, Ash turned off the television. "Okay, guys. Let's see who can do a better accent. Say 'I'd like to see the ruby amulet y'all have in the vault.'"

Chaos sat up straight. "I would like to see the ruby amulet you...yah...yawl have in the vault."

"Uh-uh. That was terrible." Ember wrinkled her nose. "Let's hear yours, Mayhem."

The sound of my name on her lips sent a warm shiver up my spine. I cleared my throat and leaned back casually, resting my arm on the back of the couch. Texans seemed to speak slowly, in a relaxed manner, and I did my best to emulate the character Miles had specified.

"Ah'd lahke ta see the ruby amulet y'all have in the vault."

Ember blinked, surprise lifting her brow. "That was an almost perfect Matthew McConaughey impression."

Ash nodded her appreciation. "It was fecking fabulous. Say 'alright, alright, alright.'"

I repeated the phrase in the actor's accent, trying my best to imitate his mannerisms.

Ember patted my thigh, my stomach clenching with her touch. "I think we've found our Boyd Anderson. But you'll have to behave yourself. No using your mind-melting magic, okay?"

I leveled my gaze on hers. "I will do anything you want, give you anything you desire. I am here to serve you, my feisty fire witch."

Her lips parted, the lower one trembling before she pressed them together and swallowed hard. "Well, then... I think we should call it a night."

CHAPTER 17

EMBER

I know, I know. I had just told Mayhem I needed time to process all the new emotions flooding my system, but I couldn't lie... Hearing this powerful man, this *Prince of Hell*, say he was here to serve me turned me on to no end.

That was one emotion I didn't need to process.

He had a cocky attitude and anger issues, yet he'd been so gentle massaging my shoulders. I'd been on the receiving end of a back rub from a man a few times, but Mayhem was the only one who paid attention to the task, actually feeling the tightness in my muscles and working out the sore spots. Everyone else just squeezed a few times, hoping it would be enough to get them into my pants.

Mayhem seemed to care about more than my vagina, which made me feel all warm and fuzzy inside, and *that* was an emotion I needed time to process. Warm and fuzzy I was not.

At least, I didn't used to be.

After we cleaned up our dinner mess, Ash and Chaos retired to their room, leaving me alone in the kitchen with Mayhem.

"How is your headache?" he asked like he was genuinely concerned.

"It's better, thanks to you." I drew my lower lip between my teeth, and his gaze slid down to my mouth. "I guess we should head to bed."

"Indeed." His eyes met mine, and we stood there, staring, his gaze penetrating all the way to my soul. "Shall I sleep in Cinder's room again?"

I opened my mouth to say yes, but the word didn't make it past my throat. Instead, I stepped toward him, resting my palms against his chest and rising to my toes to kiss him. His lips were soft against mine, the facial hair around them more like silk than the coarseness I would have expected had I not already kissed him today.

What happened this morning felt like weeks ago. Logically, I should not have been falling this hard, this fast, for anyone, much less a demon prince. Yet, there I was, sliding my arms around his shoulders and leaning into him.

He rested his hands on my hips, opening to me,

brushing his tongue to mine before pulling back, his eyes searching mine. "You said you needed time."

"I know. I do." But time for what? To come to terms with the fact that I was fated to him? Really, there weren't any terms I *could* come to. Fate was fate, and fighting it would only lead to trouble. I should listen to my heart. The heart always knew what was right, but my brain wouldn't shut the eff up.

If I allowed myself to go all in, I would get my heart broken. This budding relationship had a hard and fast expiration date, and I wasn't sure I'd survive the ending.

"Fate is a fickle bitch." Emotion tightened my chest, one fist around my heart, the other squeezing my throat.

"Perhaps. It's possible fate brought us together simply to teach us a lesson before pulling us apart." He cupped my face in his hands. "That isn't what this feels like, though."

"But we will be torn apart. It's the only way to set the world right."

He stroked my cheek with his thumb. "I would gladly destroy this world and mine if it meant I could spend eternity with you."

See? That right there should have been a massive red flag to a light witch, but it wasn't. Not to this light witch, anyway. Never had I ever been desired—loved?—this fiercely. *Hecate have mercy on my soul.*

"I don't want you to destroy anything but my family's curse."

"I know." He tucked my hair behind my ear.

"Can I have your promise that you won't?"

"No." He held my gaze, studying my reaction. "I will not make a promise to you that I can't keep."

Was that another red flag? Or was it a green one? My stomach was doing this weird combination of fluttering, turning, and clenching, and I had no idea how to interpret it.

"You could keep it if you wanted to."

He slid his hands to my shoulders. "If anyone causes you pain, they will pay. I will not be able to stop myself. You are mine to protect."

"I can take care of myself." Good goddess, these emotions needed to chill the eff out.

A smile curved his lips. "I know. It's one of the many things I love about you."

Add flip-flops to my stomach's gymnastics show. "How can you call this love when you've only known me a week?"

"My soul has known yours since the beginning of time. Our energies were created as one, then separated, half into my realm, half into yours. My darkness has been searching for your light since the moment we split, and now that I've found you, we are whole once again."

His words sank deep into my soul, resonating in my being and making themselves at home.

"I call this love because there is no other single word that can convey this connection to you. Even love does not do our bond justice, but there is no other way to describe it."

"You've done a pretty good job." I clutched the back of his neck, pulling him down until his mouth met mine.

An *mmm* vibrated across his lips as he slid his arms around me, pulling me close. Whether or not this was love, I couldn't say, but I was tired of thinking. My mind was exhausted from trying to decipher my emotions, so I gave up.

I wanted Mayhem. He wanted me. Why shouldn't we act on it?

I kissed him harder, reveling in the heat of his mouth and the sensation of his rock-hard dick pressing into my stomach. When I nipped his bottom lip between my teeth, he groaned and lifted me onto the countertop.

I spread my legs so he could fit between them, and he pulled me closer, pressing his groin against me and kissing me like I was his last breath of air. He slid one hand up my back to fist in my hair while he cupped my breast with the other.

With a tug, he angled my neck, giving himself better

access to the sensitive spot beneath my ear. His lips grazed my skin before his tongue slipped out, gliding up to my earlobe and raising goosebumps on my arms.

"You belong to me." His breath whispered across my ear, making me shiver in a good way.

"You've got it backwards." I popped the button on his jeans. "*You* belong to *me*." I reached into his pants and wrapped my hand around his dick.

His breath came out as a hiss. "Yes, I do."

"You'll do anything I want you to." I stroked his length twice, my mouth watering at the contrast of silky-soft skin on his rock-hard girth.

He inhaled deeply, pressing his forehead to mine and closing his eyes. "I will. Anything."

"Take me to bed."

"It will be my pleasure." He lifted me from the counter and carried me to my bedroom, kicking the door shut behind him before lowering my feet to the floor.

I cast a quick silencing spell and pushed him toward the bed, shoving his pants to the floor on the way. He kicked them aside and grabbed the back of his shirt, pulling it forward, over his head, and tossing it onto the pile.

Heat pooled below my navel as I took in the sheer perfection of Mayhem. The dark hair sprinkled across his muscular chest made my fingers twitch to touch him, to follow the trail down his defined abs and take his length into my hand...and then into my mouth. Yes, he was a demon, but he could have been a god.

His deep purple eyes glinted with desire, and when I licked my lips, his pupils dilated.

"Sit down." I pressed my palm to his chest, and he obeyed, sinking onto the edge of the bed and spreading his legs.

Resting a hand on each of his muscular thighs, I lowered to my knees and looked up at him. His lips parted like he wanted to say something, but when I flicked out my tongue, licking him from bottom to top, his words turned into a moan.

I circled my tongue around his tip before grazing it with my teeth. That earned me a groan as he gripped the edge of the bed. I took his first two inches into my mouth and wrapped my hand around his base.

His stomach clenched as I sucked, taking him in deeper, and the tips of his talons began to protrude from his fingers. I rested one hand on top of his, and he curled it into a fist. "I'm sorry."

"Don't be," I whispered against his dick, turning his skin to gooseflesh as I licked him. "I love having this effect on you."

He relaxed his fingers, and as I took him into my mouth as deeply as I could, his talons extended even more. He moaned as I sucked him, and when he rested his clawed hand atop my head, moisture pooled between my legs.

A deep growl rumbled in his chest, and with a sharp intake of air, he tugged my hair, pulling me away from his dick. The purple of his irises bled outward, undulating as it overtook the white, making my pulse sprint.

His nostrils flared, his eyes narrowing, his expression that of a predator about to devour his prey. A trill of fear shimmied up my spine, my body reacting to the imaginary danger of being stared down by a demon.

But this wasn't just any demon. Mayhem was *my* demon, and he was about to make me *his* witch.

I rose to my feet, instinctively taking a step back. Adrenaline coursed through me, heightening my arousal, and as he stood, looming over me, I unbuttoned my jeans, my pulse whooshing in my ears as I shoved them to the floor.

He stepped forward, splaying his fingers. My stomach flipped as I took off my shirt and bra. Another step toward me, and he glided the dull side of a talon across my stomach before hooking the sharp side into my underwear and ripping them off with a flick of his wrist.

My heart pounded so hard, I could see its rhythm in my chest.

With a hand on either side of me, he boxed me in, pinning me against the wall. A hint of tusks protruded from his gums, making me tremble in an oh-so-good way.

I clutched his dick, stroking it as I licked my lips. "I'm not afraid of you."

I fully expected him to tell me I should be, but he didn't. His gaze wandered over my face, pausing on my mouth before returning to my eyes. "Good. I don't want you to be. This is who I am."

"I know." I brushed my lips to his and slipped my tongue between the tips of his tusks. They hadn't fully extended, and they didn't hinder the kiss at all. In fact, they turned me on even more.

He moaned into my mouth, pressing his body to mine, and I wrapped my arms around him, holding him there. "I don't think I can hold back much longer," he said. "I need you."

"Then take me." Because I was about to explode with desire.

He pulled away, grabbing my hips and bending me over the bed before tracing his claws down my back. Goosebumps pricked every inch of my skin, and I spread my legs wider, bracing my arms on the mattress as he rubbed his tip against my wet folds.

I moaned, moving my hips toward him to take him inside. A pleasurable ache expanded in my core as he filled me completely, and he reached a human hand around my waist to stroke my clit.

Electricity pinged through my body, setting my nerves ablaze. He slid out until only his tip remained, and again I leaned into him, taking him deeper. Countering my movement, he pushed into me, circling his fingers on my sensitive nub as he ground his hips against me.

A masculine grunt emanated from his chest. He pumped his hips, a taloned hand clutching my shoulder while he rubbed me with human fingers. An orgasm coiled inside me, the delicious friction of his every move sending me closer and closer to the edge until my entire world exploded.

Ecstasy surged through my body, setting my soul on fire. I cried out in pleasure, shouting his name, and he growled, slamming into me three more times before sinking in so deep he penetrated my very being.

He huffed heavy breaths and placed his elbows on the bed, both his hands in their human form. Resting his front against my back, he nuzzled into my neck before pressing a kiss to the side of my head. "Did I hurt you?"

I laughed and turned, craning my neck to see him. "Quite the opposite."

His eyes and teeth had returned to normal, and with one more heavy breath, he pulled out and collapsed onto the mattress next to me. "You are everything."

I had no idea what to say to that, so I climbed under the covers and lifted the top of the blanket, inviting him in. He lay on his side, and I snuggled against him as the little spoon, clutching the arm he wrapped around me.

Even more emotions built in the core of my being, pinging off each other and swirling in a messy cyclone inside my soul. None of this was going like I'd planned. It felt as if I'd been hijacked by a person who knew how to *feel*. The problem was I didn't know what to do about it.

So I just lay there, staring straight ahead into the darkness and trying not to think about anything.

"I love you, Ember," he whispered against my hair.

I pretended to be asleep.

CHAPTER 18

EMBER

"Do we really think a New York auction house is going to notice if 'Boyd' isn't wearing cowboy boots?" Ash stood in the kitchen, pouring premixed binding spells into a series of small glass bottles. Her hand twitched, and she knocked a bottle over, spilling the contents. "I have got to find out where that New Orleans coven gets their capsules. These bottles make me feel like a boomer."

"With the heavy accent Mayhem will be laying on them, I think they will." I pulled up the map app and entered New York City as the destination before adding 'cowboy boots' to the search. "There are two places to get them between here and there."

"Boots aren't cheap." She corked the bottles and added them to her bag o' spells.

I pocketed my phone. "I'm doing what Miles tells us to. We can't give them any reason to suspect Mayhem isn't a Texas oil baron who dabbles in occult antiques as his guilty pleasure."

Chaos rinsed the bowl Ash had used and dried it with a dishtowel. "Is a Texan wearing cowboy attire not equivalent to a Salem witch wearing a pointy hat?"

"Not at all," Miles said as he stepped through the door. "Boots are as common in Texas as beanies are here."

Mayhem joined us in the kitchen, fresh from his shower, a lock of damp hair curling onto his forehead. A flitting sensation formed in my stomach, and I brushed the strands into place before they could drip onto his skin.

I'd kept up my charade of not hearing him say he loved me, and thankfully, he hadn't mentioned it since. I did allow myself the luxury of snuggling into his warm embrace for a while when we woke up. But then we had to face reality and prepare for our scariest mission to date.

Battling beasties I could handle, but humans... Sometimes they were the real monsters, and unfortunately, I wasn't allowed to chop off their heads.

That didn't mean I had to leave my sword behind. My back scabbard lay on the counter, the blade sheathed in fireproof leather. Mayhem caressed the rosewood handle and traced the texture of the skull pommel.

"Whoever built this weapon for you had the gift of foresight," he said, tapping the skull for emphasis. "Unless you requested this design. If so, perhaps you have a latent gift."

A bark of laughter rolled up from my chest. "I wish." I cleared my throat. "My mom had it forged for me. The creator had free reign in the design."

"You can't take weapons inside," Miles said. "They'll have metal detectors and a body scanner."

"I'll leave her in the van. Is everything set up?"

He nodded. "Shade is outside, watching the equipment. We're ready when you are."

I picked up my sword and a bundle of knives wrapped in thick fabric. "Are you done, Ash? Let's head out."

"Yep." She slung her bag over her shoulder, and we filed outside.

Thick gray clouds blanketed the sky, the air so chilly and damp that I shivered. Mayhem wrapped his arm around me, and though I appreciated his warmth, I stepped out of his embrace. No way in hell was I going to lose myself like Ash had. I could imagine the devastation she would feel when the demons returned to the Underworld, and I refused to expose myself to that kind of turmoil.

At the van, I opened the sliding side door and

stowed my weapons in the hidey hole. The guys had removed half of the way back seat to set up a makeshift base of operations. They'd zip-tied a folding table against the wall, and a plastic case with who-knew-what kind of equipment occupied the floor beneath it.

A monitor, also zip-tied into place, sat atop the table, and the power cable running behind it plugged into a battery pack the size of...well, I suppose it was a car battery.

I opened the driver's side door and cringed at the shattered windshield as I climbed into the seat. "At least the imp had the courtesy to only smash the passenger side."

Mayhem took shotgun and ran his finger over the inside of the glass. "The damage is confined to the outer layer."

"Thank the goddess for that." I started the engine.

"If Hecate is holding the veil together," he said, "I doubt she had anything to do with the imp."

"Silly demon. It's just an expression. Load up, guys."

My team climbed into the van, and I pulled onto the road. "It's about two hours to the boot store, and then another two after that. What's the rest of the plan?" I glanced at Miles in the rearview mirror, and he straightened.

"I was able to hack into their security system last

night. Everyone will have earpieces so we can communicate." He held up a tiny piece of silicone. "Once the amulet is in your sight, I can loop the security feed so everything looks normal. They'll return it to the vault after you see it, so it'll be up to you and Mayhem to swipe it before they do."

"I will do my best to only render them unconscious," Mayhem said. "Any casualties will be unintentional."

I gave him the side eye. "There won't be any casualties. Why do you think Ash mixed so many binding spells? We freeze them, take the amulet, and get the hell out of New York before anyone realizes what happened."

He raised his brows. "You've thought this through."

"This is the most planning I think I've done in my entire life." I laughed. "Weird, isn't it?"

"Indeed." He studied my profile, a grin lifting one corner of his mouth. "I can't decide if I like this side of you or not."

"Neither can I."

We rode in silence once we got the plan hashed out, which I normally would have appreciated. With only the radio and the low drone of the wheels on the pavement to occupy my thoughts, my mind decided it was time to mull over my Mayhem predicament. Again.

The problem was...every thought I had about the situation circled back to the inevitable ending. His time in this realm was finite. Sure, we could try to figure out some way to resummon the demons without damaging the veil, but I could never ask him to give up his home and everything he knew just to live a normal, nearly mundane life in our quiet little town.

Honestly, I wasn't sure how *I* could endure normal if we made it through this ordeal. Before our parents summoned the first demon, we didn't get much action in Salem. Not compared to the past few months, anyway. I'd always jumped at the chance to send a beastie back where it belonged, but sometimes we'd go days without any action.

And Mayhem... He was royalty in the Underworld. Hell, he was on a first-name basis with Lucifer *and* Hecate. No way would he want to deal with a humdrum life in the earthly realm.

And I sure as hell wasn't moving to his side of the veil.

"Your destination is on the right," my phone declared, pulling me from my thought spiral. *Hallelujah.*

I parked in the lot and killed the engine. "Time to cowboy up."

Mayhem smiled slowly, his newly learned drawl stretching out his words. "Alright, alright, alright."

"Don't say that, and don't say 'yee-haw.'" Miles pinched the bridge of his nose. "*That* is the equivalent of a witch wearing a pointy hat in Salem."

"Noted," Mayhem said, his voice returning to normal.

My team waited in the van while Mayhem and I went inside. A bell chimed above the door, signaling our arrival, and the shopkeeper, a squat man with salt-and-pepper hair, rosy cheeks, and a nametag that read George, scurried out from behind the counter. "Hello. How can I help you?"

"I need..." Mayhem started, practicing his accent.

"You need cowboy boots." George's gaze dropped to the combat-style boots he currently wore. "Size twelve? I've got just what you need."

We followed him to the boot section, and he gestured for us to sit in the plush chairs across from the display. "You look like an ostrich man. Do you have a particular color in mind? Black. I'll be right back."

Mayhem frowned as George disappeared into a back room. "He asks questions but does not wait for answers."

"He's good at his job." I patted his thigh, and he inhaled sharply before taking my hand and kissing it.

"Perhaps I wanted brown snakeskin." His warm breath danced across my fingers.

"Did you?" I tugged from his grasp and wiped my sweaty palms on my jeans.

"No, he was correct. I wonder if he's full human or something other."

Before I could explain how retail workers developed a sense for what their customers needed, without using magic, George returned with two boxes. He sat on a stool and reached for Mayhem's foot. My demon allowed the man to remove his boot and put the new one on, which was weird as all get out at first.

Then I remembered he was a prince. Lesser demons probably did his bidding on the daily back home.

The boot George had chosen had a brown heel, square toe, and a red flame pattern on the upper part. Hmm. Maybe this guy did have a little "something other" running through his veins.

Mayhem walked the length of the carpet and returned to his seat. "These will do."

George smiled triumphantly and rested his hand on the other unopened box. "I knew those were the ones. I'll put these back in a minute, but first, you'll need some bootcut jeans."

He tilted his head, eying Mayhem's belt and t-shirt. "If you're trying to get back to your roots, you'll need a belt and shirt too. Or do you already have clothes at home?"

"I—" Mayhem began.

"You haven't lived in New England long, and your wife has been dressing you. Meet me at the fitting room, and I'll gather what you need." George tucked the box beneath his arm and strode toward the men's clothing.

I wasn't keen on the wife part, but yeah, I had been dressing my demon. "Definitely something other."

We waited outside the dressing room, and George returned with starched black jeans, a black leather belt with a huge silver buckle, and a black button-up. Mayhem put them on, and everything fit perfectly.

I focused on George's aura, trying to sense any type of magic he might possess, but he seemed as mundane as Chief Higgins. If he was a magical being, the power was either multi-generationally diluted or he'd cast one helluva shrouding spell to hide it.

George gathered Mayhem's old clothes and boots and put them in a bag before ringing up our purchase. "That'll be nine hundred fifty-three dollars and seventy-six cents, please. Cash or card? Card."

I choked on my own spit. A thousand dollars for one outfit? Damn, cowboying was expensive. "Maybe we should see the other pair of boots? Do you have anything less pricey?"

George's brow furrowed, his nostrils flaring slightly as a tiny bit of the something other sparkled in his aura. "This is what he needs. Your choice of clothing for yourself will be fine, but he must wear this."

The magic dissipated as quickly as it had formed,

and I dug my credit card out of my wallet. Whatever kind of being George was, he was magically adamant my Prince of Hell had to wear this exact outfit. Who was I to question someone else's ability?

George's smile returned, and he tapped my card against the reader before handing it back to me. The register made a *duh-dun* sound, and he frowned. "I'm afraid your card has been declined. Do you have another payment method? Not with you. In your car, perhaps? Yes. The gentleman will wait with me while you call your friends on the phone. Off you go by the window. We have terrible reception in here." He had the audacity to make a shooing motion with his hand.

My teeth clicked audibly, my hands curling into fists. "What are you?"

He tapped his nametag. "I'm George. This is my shop. If you try to leave, I'll tell you to stop."

My lips pursed, sharp pain shooting from my jaw to my temple, thanks to how hard I ground my teeth. His rhyming cadence made it sound like he'd cast a spell, but the wording was off. *What a weirdo.*

If we weren't pressed for time, I would rip into this guy and make him reveal his identity. But time was the one thing we didn't have, so I turned on my heel and marched toward the window, fuming as I opened a video call with my sister.

"Uh oh." Ash held the phone in front of her so I could see everyone in the van. "What happened?"

"A thousand dollars," I whisper shouted. "A *grand* for one stupid cowboy outfit, and my card was declined. You didn't mention how expensive this costume would be."

Miles held up his hands. "What kind of boots did he pick?"

"Ostrich. Does anyone have a spare grand lying around?"

"Oh, those are expensive. Leather would be cheaper," Miles said. "But 'Boyd' wouldn't wear cheap."

"Even if he would, we can't get leather." I glanced over my shoulder and found George enticing Mayhem with a case of gold watches. "Just the clothes, Boyd. I'll get you a watch for Christmas."

Ash scrunched her face. "Why can't you get leather?"

I lowered my voice. "Because George is *something*, and he insists Mayhem needs ostrich boots and a whole outfit to match. And I would like to throttle him for telling me to shoo."

She opened the van door. "We'll come inside. I might have room on my credit card, and if not, I say this is a *for the greater good* moment."

"You're right. It is for the greater good. Screw George—if that's really even his name. Come inside and do your mind thing so we can get this shitshow on the road." I ended the call and returned to the counter, taking Mayhem's hand to stop him from trying on a silver bracelet shaped like the ouroboros.

"You didn't tell me your lovely wife's name." George drummed his fingertips together, and I could have sworn faint sparks of magic danced between them.

"You can call me Elenore," I said before Mayhem could tell him my real name.

According to lore, the fae could gain control of a person if they knew their real name. Obviously, that was bogus or the scouts and soldiers would've been demanding our names every chance they got. But the phrase *a named thing is a tamed thing* existed for a reason. Some kind of being had that power, and I didn't care to find out if our shopkeeper was that kind.

"Hmm." George narrowed his eyes at me before opening the bracelet and holding it toward Mayhem. "Try it on. It's yours, free of charge."

"No." I grabbed Mayhem's arm, yanking him away from the counter. "Change into your normal clothes. We'll buy the boots elsewhere."

He reached for the bag, but it disappeared from the counter before he could grab it. George slapped the bracelet on his wrist. The snake writhed, slithering in a circle and chomping on its own tail.

"Ha! I've got you!" George bounced on his toes, clapping like an imbecile. "Two witches for the price of one."

Mayhem blinked and shook his head as if coming out of a daze. He pulled on the bracelet, trying to unlatch it, but the snake bit its tail harder. His eyes widened as he turned to me. "Run."

I bolted for the door.

"Stop," George said, and I froze, unable to move forward.

I strained against the magic, but an invisible force field stopped me from reaching the exit. I could move backward, deeper into the store, but it would take one hell of an unraveling spell to break through this kind of magic.

The bell above the door chimed as Ash and Chaos stepped through. Her brow furrowed, and she looked from left to right, standing on her toes to see over the racks.

I stood right in front of her, but she couldn't see me.

"Ember?" she called, and my heart plopped into my stomach.

"Emberrrr..." My name dripped from George's tongue as a blanket of magic wrapped around me.

A named thing is a tamed thing...

CHAPTER 19
MAYHEM

The ouroboros encircling my wrist was a trap. I could see that now, too little, too late. The being who called himself George had tricked me from the moment I stepped into the store. He had fooled Ember at first, as well, but she'd begun seeing through his charade...also too late.

I gripped the bracelet and pulled with all my might, but the harder I tried to remove it, the tighter it became. "What is this?"

A maniacal laugh emanated from George's throat. "Witch leash. I don't need your real name. You'll come when I call and do what I say. Such is the way for those who can't pay."

He waved his arm, inviting my brother and his witch into our plane. Ash gasped, pressing a hand to her chest.

"Turn around, and walk out the door," I said, but they didn't listen.

Instead, Chaos took Ash's hand and focused on George. "We're in a hurry. You'll allow us to leave with the clothing, free of charge."

George laughed again. "Four witches! Father will be pleased."

Interesting. It seemed our aura shrouds fooled the insolent being. He had no idea we were demons. It also seemed my brother's mind control ability was useless against this being.

Chaos glared at him. "We are leaving and taking the clothing with us."

"No, no. No one is leaving. Because you can't pay, you have to stay."

Ash attempted to step backward, but an invisible wall stopped her retreat. "What are you?"

He tapped his nametag. "I'm George. This is my store."

She crossed her arms. "Not who. What."

"He's George," Ember said, her arms hanging slack at her sides. "We're going to stay here now."

"The hell we are." Ash gathered a fireball in her hand and lifted her arm to throw it at George.

Ember countered her, summoning her own fire and hurling it at her sister. The flames slammed into Ash's chest and billowed around her before dissipating as if they'd never existed.

Ash's mouth dropped open. "Seriously, Em?" She threw her fireball at her sister, the effect identical on her.

"Fire witches! What fun." George bounced and clapped. "Oh, I know. Let's have a girl fight."

Ember glowered at her sister, stalking toward her with her fists clenched. Ash tried to retreat, but the magical wall stopped her. Ember clutched her shoulders and shoved her to the ground.

"I'm not going to fight you." Ash crab walked backward. "We need to leave."

"We're staying here." Ember lunged, landing atop her sister and punching the side of her face.

"Stop," Chaos boomed. He grabbed Ember's arm and hauled her up, but she turned on him, slamming her fists into his stomach. He lifted her, and she kicked, her arms flailing as her face reddened with anger.

"Get your witch under control," he said.

If I moved to help him restrain her, George would see I was no witch. His witch leash might have tethered me to him, but he could not control me like he did Ember. I needed to keep up my charade long enough to learn his name. Only then could I free my witch from his control.

I crossed my arms to feign obstinance and sent a pulse of my magic into her. I could almost feel my mark heating on her arm as I reached into her psyche.

Her magic countered mine instantly, and she stilled, her body relaxing as she scratched her head.

"We don't need to fight," she said. "Violence never solves anything."

Chaos released his hold, and she offered a hand to Ash, helping her to her feet. She ran her fingers over the red spot she'd made on Ash's cheek. "Oof. That's going to leave a mark."

"Ya think?" Ash took a jar of salve from her bag and spread it over the impending bruise.

"What spell is this that defeats my command?" George fisted his hands on his hips. "Not a spell. A connection. A shared magic." He cocked his head at me. "What are you?"

"We asked you first." Ash returned the jar to her bag.

"He's George," Ember said. "This is his store."

Rage billowed in the pit of my stomach. My beast clawed to the surface, my talons and horns growing to their full size as I glared at the being.

"This is his store." Ember put her hands on my chest. "I'm going to live with him."

"No, my witch. You are not." I stepped away from her, and my beast took control.

The new shirt and jeans ripped to shreds as I grew, my muscles building, protruding until all humanness ceased to exist. Teeth turned to tusks, my feet to hooves, yet the bracelet conformed to my size.

I stalked to the being, grabbing him by the throat and yanking him over the counter. "Release her," I growled, "or I will kill you."

"Can't be killed," he squeaked. "Demon!"

"Don't hurt George." Ember clutched my arm and tugged. "Put him down."

I tightened my grip. George wheezed, the shroud he'd placed on himself and the store slipping away, revealing a horror to rival the Sixth Circle of Hell. At least a dozen emaciated bodies lined the wall, their arms shackled above their heads. Their eyes and cheeks had sunken in, their pallor an ashy green, their mouths open in silent screams.

"My sisters," Ember said, her voice filled with fondness as she circled her arm around Ash's biceps. "This is Ash. We'll be joining you soon."

"Ashhhhhh..." The moment he uttered her name, her eyes glazed.

"Very soon," she said.

Shade and Miles approached from the parking lot, so I slammed George against the door, holding it closed while Chaos turned the lock.

"Release them," I said again.

His face grew purple. He clawed at my talons and kicked, attempting to wiggle free.

"Put him down, brother." Chaos placed a hand on my shoulder. "He can't free them if he's dead."

I lowered him to the ground, releasing my hold.

"Can't be killed." He laughed and tiptoed toward the bodies. "Space for you here." He gestured to an empty spot along the wall. "If you can't pay, you have to stay."

Our witches started toward him, but we put our arms around them. "What are you?" Chaos asked, though I had a feeling he knew the answer, as did I.

"He's George," the witches said in unison.

"I'm George." The being tapped his nametag.

"That's not your name," Chaos said. "You're a Formorian."

Surprise widened his eyes, and he clutched his hands in front of his chest. "Formorians are extinct. Fae vanquished them all." His nose twitched, his true form threatening to break through his disguise.

"I thought so too, but here you are." Chaos crossed his arms. "What is your name, Formorian?"

"He's just George." Ember patted my arm.

"I'm just George. No Formorian here."

"No." I loosened my grip on Ember, though I still held her firmly. "He's no Formorian. I'd call him an imp at best."

"An imp!" His eyes turned yellow, his pupils narrowing into vertical slits as his nose elongated into a snout. "Formorians are better than imps. Better than any demon from Hell."

"So you are a Formorian," Chaos said.

George lifted his head, puffing out his chest. "I am

a son of Balor. I...whoops." He disappeared in a puff of smoke.

"I need to join my sisters." Ember struggled against me.

"We must get them out of here." I rushed for the exit and turned the lock, throwing the door open and charging at the threshold.

The bracelet tightened on my wrist, and the sensation of a thousand thorns raking across my skin slowed my escape. I pushed through, as if walking through a tarpit. Ember cried out in agony, clawing at my arms and writhing in my grip. A popping sound echoed around us as we passed through the magical ward, and the pain ceased as quickly as it had begun. Ember sighed with relief, her body going slack in my embrace.

We stood in the center of the Formorian's store.

"No." I ran for the door once more.

Again the bracelet tightened, and thorns scraped across my skin. Ember wailed. We returned to the center of the store.

"What in Lucifer's name?" Chaos stared at me, bewilderment contorting his expression.

"He trapped me." I held up my arm, showing him the ouroboros encircling my wrist.

My brother merely sighed, yet I could feel his disappointment dripping from the breath he exhaled. "You fell for his guise."

"I was…" An idiot. It wasn't his guise that had fooled me. No, it was my own folly that got me…that got us…into this predicament. I'd gotten caught up in my emotions, enjoying this mundane shopping experience with the woman I loved.

My focus had been so pinpointed on the moment, I hadn't noticed there was nothing mundane about it.

"You must get them out." I clutched Ember's shoulders and pushed her toward him. "Take them to safety."

"What about you?" He extended one arm, taking my witch into his embrace.

"I will find a way out." I held his gaze with conviction. Ember's life was worth far more than my own. I would remain in this shop of horrors for eternity if it meant my witch would be free. "Guard her with your life."

"I will." Chaos stepped through the door, and the witches screamed.

In an instant, both women reappeared in the center of the store. Chaos stood just past the threshold, with Miles and Shade flanking him.

"What the hell is going on?" Shade clutched a knife in each hand.

"My sisters." Ember gripped Ash's hand as they sank against the wall adjacent to the bodies.

I spun in a circle, searching with my eyes and my

magical senses. George was nowhere to be found. "A Formorian has trapped us."

Miles frowned. "Aren't they extinct? I thought the fae wiped them out eons ago."

"We thought so too," Chaos said. "It was the one thing both demons and the fae agreed upon. Formorians were a blight to all the realms, so we aided them in their battle."

I watched the women intently. No chains magically appeared to bind them. "This one says he's a son of Balor."

"Which means he is a prince," Chaos said. "He's as powerful as us."

"Can you vanquish him?" Miles asked. "Will that dissolve his spell?"

"No. I have dealt with these creatures before." I moved toward the door, keeping Ember and Ash in my sight. "Their magic holds, even if they are vanquished. We must find him and learn his name. Only then can we force him to release the women."

"We're coming in." Shade moved for the door.

Chaos grabbed his arm. "Do not, under any circumstances, use real names."

"That is how he trapped the women," I said. "If he learns your names, you'll be joining the other bodies chained to the wall."

"Bodies?" Miles stepped inside and gulped. "Holy shit."

"Indeed." I peered around the clothing racks. "M, watch the women. If the Formorian reappears, do not allow him to bind them. And feel free to rough him up if you must. I plan to make him beg for vanquishment."

"On it." He pulled out his phone and typed on the screen. "You said he's a son of Balor, right? I'll see if I can find his name."

"Good." I stalked toward the shoe area. "Show yourself, Formorian."

"He's just George," Ember said. "This is his store."

I growled. How could I, a Prince of Hell, have allowed this to happen? I had no doubt my brothers would have seen through this ruse the moment they set foot inside the store. But not I... Perhaps I deserved their incessant ridicule, after all.

Even Ember saw through the charade before I did. She deserved a mate who could protect her. She deserved better than me.

"It's going to take a minute." Miles held his phone near the window. "The reception in here is terrible."

I eyed the door to the back of the shop. "I will find him."

My fists clenched as tightly as my talons would allow, I kicked the door open, making it bounce off the wall with the impact. George squealed, the sound of his invisible feet scampering across the floor registering to my left.

Chaos and Shade followed me inside the storage room, and we fanned out, searching for the insolent creature. George grunted, and a shelving unit filled with boxes rocked on its base.

"Your race went extinct for a reason." I crept down the aisle. "You cannot defeat us."

"Demons didn't vanquish my kind. Fae did that." His voice sounded from my right, so I turned down the next aisle.

The shelving unit rocked again, and this time, it tipped over. Boxes scattered across the floor, the shoes inside them tumbling out as it crashed into me.

I caught the brunt of it with my shoulder, and I stumbled before pushing the unit upright. Kicking the boxes out of my way, I rushed for the next aisle. Shade and Chaos stood at the opposite end, trapping the invisible pest between us.

"Son of Balor, show yourself," I said.

"You can't make me!"

Shade grunted, clutching his abdomen and doubling over, bracing himself with the shelf. When he lifted his hand, blood dripped from his palm.

CHAPTER 20
MAYHEM

"Son of a bitch," Shade ground out.

"No! Son of Balor." The voice came from deeper in the room.

"Can you freeze him?" I asked as we rushed toward the sound.

Shade stopped, still bent forward and clutching his stomach, and pulled a bottled spell from his pocket. "If we can find him."

Blood soaked his shirt, and he paled. "The bastard got me good."

"Not a bastard." The *slap, slap, slap* of his shoes on the tile moved toward the showroom door. "Dad was king. Mom was queen."

A thud sounded from the aisle littered with boxes. The door swung open and slammed shut. I charged for it, but the handle wouldn't turn.

"Those who can't pay have to stay." George laughed maniacally from the other side. "Time to drain my witches."

"Over my rotting corpse." I slammed my shoulder against the door, but it wouldn't budge.

"Step aside." Chaos braced himself to break down the door. His brow furrowed, and he paused before turning the knob. The door swung open easily.

"It's this damn bracelet." I hooked a talon beneath the offending silver and pulled. The snake writhed and tightened, taking more of its tail into its mouth.

Shade stumbled through the door. I reached a hand out, testing the Formorian's spell, and my arm passed the threshold. I stepped through as if there were no spell at all. His magic was waning. Good.

Miles stood in front of the women, a knife in one hand, his phone in the other. "Sha—?" He closed his mouth before he could finish the name. Concern furrowed his brow, and he cut his gaze between the now visible creature and the shadow witch.

"It's a gut wound. He'll bleed out slowly." George wrinkled his pig-like snout, sniffing the air. "Move, witch. Father needs to eat."

I lunged for the Formorian. He disappeared in a blink and reformed behind Miles, crouching over Ember and pressing his snout to her mouth. Miles spun, swinging his knife. George disintegrated again, reforming in an instant.

Chaos moved for Ash and dragged her away from the wall. She kicked and screamed, begging to return to her place amongst the corpses.

Every swing, lunge, and jab I threw at George, he dodged, returning his snout to my witch's mouth faster than anything I'd seen. Ember's pallor grew pale. Dark circles ringed her eyes as he sucked the life out of her.

Shade threw the binding spell at the creature and recited the incantation. George merely laughed and continued devouring my soulmate.

Fire ignited in my hands, licking up my arms until my entire body was ablaze. I hurled a ball of hellfire at the beast, hitting him in the back of his head.

He squealed like the pig he was and spun to face me. "Hellfire burns. Don't do that."

He waved his arm, and a wall began to grow from the floor. He strained with the effort, the grimace contorting his face making him look like a clone of Balor.

I shot a stream of hellfire from my palms, blasting the growing wall. Fire billowed around it, lighting a rack of shirts ablaze.

"Brother..." Chaos laid a heavy hand on my shoulder. "You'll burn the place down."

"Our witches are immune to fire." The blaze leaped from the shirts to a shelf of folded jeans. "M, take S outside and tend to his wounds. I'm ending this now."

Ash wiggled from his grasp and returned to her spot along the wall.

"If you vanquish him, our witches will be stuck in their trance forever." Chaos tugged my arm, lowering it as the fire consumed the wall and spread throughout the store.

"Call it back," he said. "There is another way." He held up the phone Mile's had handed him. "Angus, son of Balor."

The Formorian froze, turning to my brother. "Angus is an imbecile. He was the first of the royal family to die."

I took the phone. Twenty-three names filled the screen. I called my fire back, the flames rolling into my being, leaving charred bits of leather and fabric in its wake.

"Cormac," I growled the next name on the list.

"No, no. I'll drain them both before you guess it." He turned to Ember and pressed his snout to her mouth again.

She groaned, and my stomach wrenched. "Eachan, Duncan, Cian," I shouted.

My witch's cheeks began to sink in. A vise squeezed my heart. I swiped my thumb on the screen, scrolling to the last name on the list. "Donal, son of Balor, you will release the witches at once."

He jerked his head away from Ember, his body stiffening, a hiss escaping his mouth.

"Donal," I said again, "release the witches now."

"You...can't...make....me," he strained against the magic taking hold.

"Donal," Chaos said, his chest rumbling with his growl as he approached the Formorian. "Release them."

Ember's head lolled to the side, and she slumped to her left, leaning against Ash's shoulder.

"Turn around, Donal," I said, and he groaned, fighting my command as he faced me.

Shade collapsed behind me, and Miles grabbed Ash's bag, yanking the strap over her head as she sat there in a daze, a maddening smile plastered on her face.

Donal disappeared in a puff of smoke.

"Show yourself," my brother and I said in unison. Donal reappeared and vanished again.

Miles dragged Shade next to Ember and rummaged through the bag, cursing as he looked at bottle after bottle.

"I will not play this game, Donal," I shouted. "Show yourself and do not disappear again."

The Formorian appeared next to Ash, taking her head in his hands.

"For goddess's sake," Miles grumbled and blew a powder on the creature. "Standing tall or on your knees, in the name of the goddess, I force you, Donal, to freeze."

A wheeze escaped his throat, but this time, the magic held. I wrapped my talons around the insolent being's neck and jerked him away from the women. Ember slumped even more, falling into Ash's lap, and the vise gripping my heart nearly burst it.

"Tell me there is something in that bag to help my witch."

"I'm looking, but..." Miles turned it upside down and dumped the contents onto the floor. "I don't know. I don't know what he did to her. I..." He held up a bottle triumphantly, and hope sprung in my heart.

He turned to Shade and lifted his shirt, wincing at the three-inch puncture wound before pouring the yellow liquid onto his skin.

"Ember needs your help. Her state is dire." I kneeled in front of her, dragging the Formorian down with me.

"I know it is, but I know how to help S. I have no idea what to do for her. That's Ash's department." He recited an incantation, and Shade's bleeding slowed. "He'll need stitches."

With Donal's throat firmly in my grasp, I used my other hand to brush the hair from Ember's face. She didn't move, didn't react to my touch. "Take him, brother."

Chaos grabbed Donal's arm and hauled him up before clutching his throat. "Release the witches, Donal."

"He can't while he's frozen," Miles said.

I pulled Ember into my lap and brushed the hair from her forehead. The strands felt dry and brittle, her skin like worn leather. I laid a hand on her breast, searching for the rise and fall of her chest. It moved only slightly, her breathing slow and shallow, but she was still alive.

If she did not make it through this, I would never recover. After I burned the Formorian and shit on his ashes, I would beg Lucifer to end my life. I could not exist without my witch...and this was my fault entirely.

I should have paid attention to the signs. I should have noticed the vibration was off in this store the moment I stepped through the door. A sob rolled up from the core of my being, thickening my throat and making my eyes sting.

"I'm so sorry, my love." I kissed her withered forehead and turned my livid gaze on the motionless Formorian. "Undo your spell so he can release them."

Miles recited an undoing spell, and Donal gasped, clawing at Chaos's hand as he dangled from his grip.

"Release the witches, Donal," I growled.

"Never. I am Donal, Prince of the Formorians. My power is greater than yours."

"Release them, Donal," Chaos said.

The creature continued his struggle.

"Donal, let them go." Miles threaded a needle through Shade's wound.

The shadow witch winced and spoke through clenched teeth. "Do it, Donal. Let them go."

The Formorian groaned.

"Let them go," the four of us repeated again, and Donal let out a breath, his body going slack.

Ash gasped and blinked, confusion clouding her eyes as she took in the scene. "What...? Ember!" She crawled toward us and clutched her sister's hand in hers. "Oh, my goddess."

Ash held her fingers beneath Ember's nose. "She's barely breathing. What did you do to her?"

I gazed at my feisty witch, Chaos's command to answer her barely registering in my senses as my beautiful warrior exhaled a final breath.

ALSO BY CARRIE PULKINEN

Fire Witches of Salem Series

Chaos and Ash

Commanding Chaos

Claiming Chaos

Mayhem and Ember

Mending Mayhem

Mastering Mayhem

New Orleans Nocturnes Series

License to Bite

Shift Happens

Life's a Witch

Santa Got Run Over by a Vampire

Finders Reapers

Swipe Right to Bite

Batshift Crazy

Collection One: Books 1-3

Collection Two: Books 4 - 7

Crescent City Wolf Pack Series

Werewolves Only

Beneath a Blue Moon

Bound by Blood

A Deal with Death

A Song to Remember

Shifting Fate

Collection One: Books 1-3

Collection Two: Books 4-6

Haunted Ever After Series

Love at First Haunt

Second Chance Spirit

Third Time's a Ghost

Love and Ghosts

Love and Omens

Love and Curses

Collection One: Books 1 - 3

Collection Two: Books 4 - 6

Stand Alone Books

Flipping the Bird

Sign Steal Deliver

Azrael

Lilith

The Rest of Forever

Soul Catchers

Bewitching the Vampire

About the Author

Carrie Pulkinen is a paranormal romance author who has always been fascinated with things that go bump in the night. Of course, when you grow up next door to a cemetery, the dead (and the undead) are hard to ignore. Pair that with her passion for writing and her love of a good happily-ever-after, and becoming a paranormal romance author seems like the only logical career choice.

Before she decided to turn her love of the written word into a career, Carrie spent the first part of her professional life as a high school journalism and yearbook teacher. She loves good chocolate and bad puns, and in her free time, she likes to read, drink wine, and travel with her family.

Connect with Carrie online:
CarriePulkinen.com